STAY
FROM THAT CITY...
THEY CALL IT
CHEYENNE

Crossway Books by
STEPHEN BLY

THE STUART BRANNON WESTERN SERIES
Hard Winter at Broken Arrow Crossing
False Claims at the Little Stephen Mine
Last Hanging at Paradise Meadow
Standoff at Sunrise Creek
Final Justice at Adobe Wells
Son of an Arizona Legend

THE NATHAN T. RIGGINS WESTERN ADVENTURE SERIES
(AGES 9–14)
The Dog Who Would Not Smile
Coyote True
You Can Always Trust a Spotted Horse
The Last Stubborn Buffalo in Nevada
Never Dance with a Bobcat
Hawks Don't Say Goodbye

THE CODE OF THE WEST SERIES
It's Your Misfortune and None of My Own
One Went to Denver and the Other Went Wrong
Where the Deer and the Antelope Play
Stay Away from That City . . . They Call It Cheyenne

THE AUSTIN-STONER FILES
The Lost Manuscript of Martin Taylor Harrison
The Final Chapter of Chance McCall

CODE OF THE WEST

BOOK FOUR

STAY AWAY FROM THAT CITY... THEY CALL IT CHEYENNE

Stephen Bly

CROSSWAY BOOKS • WHEATON, ILLINOIS
A DIVISION OF GOOD NEWS PUBLISHERS

Stay Away from That City . . . They Call It Cheyenne

Copyright © 1996 by Stephen Bly

Published by Crossway Books
         a division of Good News Publishers
         1300 Crescent Street
         Wheaton, Illinois 60187

Cover illustration: Larry Selman

First printing 1996

Printed in the United States of America

Library of Congress Cataloging-in-Publication Data
Bly, Stephen A., 1944-
   Stay away from that city / Stephen Bly.
      p.   cm.—(Code of the West; bk. 4)
   I. Title   II. Series: Bly, Stephen A., 1944- Code of the West series.
PS3552.L9305 1995   813'.54—dc20   94-38680
ISBN 0-89107-890-8

8.99/5.39 *Ingram*

05	04	03	02	01	00	99	98	97	96
15	14	13	12	11	10	9	8	7	6	5	4	3	2	1

5-1-97

For
JAMES A. "BRONCO" GWINN
WAGON-BOSS

1

onday, April 2, 1883, Cheyenne, Wyoming Territory.
"Pappy's done been shot in the back down at the
Occidental, and I'm lookin' for the deputy!" The man
stood on the worn wooden porch and rolled the brim of a once-
gray felt hat that he held in his hand.

Her mouth had partially dropped open, and she stared at him
for a minute as the words sank in.

"I say, I'm sorry to disturb you so early, Mrs. Andrews. I've got
to find—"

"Oh, Mr. Hayburn, yes, of course. Deputy Andrews is down at
the I-X-L Livery looking at a new horse." Pepper reached under
her blonde hair and began to untie the apron strings at the back
of her neck. "Is . . . is Pappy dead?"

"He weren't movin' none when I ran out the door! Them
drovers and bummers are at it again. I reckon a couple of 'em were
as full of holes as a cabbage leaf in a hailstorm before Pappy ever
came in the door."

She could see the leathery worry lines around Rolly's brown
eyes, full of fear and sadness. He slapped his floppy hat on his
head and turned toward the rising sun.

"Rolly, did anyone notify Savannah yet?"

"No, ma'am. I don't think so."

Pepper hurried back inside and laid the faded gingham apron
on the bench of the grand piano that filled most of the tiny front

room. She then stepped back out to the unroofed porch. "Well, you go tell her, and I'll find Mr. Andrews."

"Eh . . . no, ma'am, I cain't do that. I . . . eh, I had to tell her last time. I reckon it's someone else's turn."

Scattered tufts of white clouds hung low and motionless in the blue Wyoming sky as if waiting for word from above to resume their westward journey.

"Oh, well, go on . . . you get Tap," Pepper urged. "I'll go tell Savannah."

"Thank ya, Mrs. Andrews. You know, it don't seem even-handed to Miz Savannah, does it? Her havin' lost them other two by bullets already."

Pepper shook her head and sighed. Then holding her gray dress above her ankles, she hurried down the worn boardwalk of 17th Street toward the Inter Ocean Hotel.

Lord, it isn't fair. She's such a lady of strong faith. How could she lose three husbands? Let him live, Lord . . . let Pappy live!

Only one man, neatly dressed and reading a paper, occupied the lavish lobby of the hotel as Pepper scurried up the wide, swooping mahogany staircase, sliding her thin left hand along the bannister. The hallway had a pleasing mingle of pipe smoke and perfume. Pepper rapped the knuckles of her ungloved hand against the polished door of Suite G.

I probably look frightful. I should have tried to comb my hair. "Savannah?"

"Go away!" a melodious but groggy voice echoed from inside the apartment.

"Savannah, it's me . . . Pepper Andrews. I must speak with you right now!"

The heavy door immediately swung open. Savannah Divide's curly auburn hair cascaded across her usually straight but now sagging shoulders. No make-up brightened her face, and the blue robe she wore draped across her in a hurried, wanton manner.

"Pappy's dead . . . isn't he?" she challenged in a totally uncharacteristic quiet voice.

Pepper glanced away from Savannah's penetrating blue eyes. "Did someone tell you?"

"No."

"All I know is that he was back-shot down at the Occidental. Mr. Hayburn said he was hurt bad, but he didn't—"

"He's dead. I just know it. Just like the others. I always know."

"Perhaps it's not . . ."

"Why do I keep marrying lawmen? Can you tell me that, Pepper Andrews?" Not waiting for an answer, Savannah staggered back into the apartment. "I'll get dressed. Is it cold out?"

"Eh, not really. The wind isn't even blowing."

"Well, it would be the first time I've lost a husband on a nice day. Drake was killed during a blizzard, and the day Quintin died the dust blew so thick you couldn't see across the street. Please wait for me, Pepper. I'd appreciate you coming along."

"Of course."

Pepper entered the well-furnished apartment. It was a stark contrast to her own little, unpainted cottage on 17th Street. She surveyed the full-length etched mirror and ran her fingers through the blonde hair that never stayed neatly tucked in her combs.

Within minutes Savannah Divide buzzed across the room and clutched Pepper's arm. The two women hurried down the stairs and out the front door of the Inter Ocean Hotel.

"You've never lost a husband yet, have you, dear?"

"Eh . . . no. Tap and I just got married in December."

"It really takes the steam out of you, that's for sure. How old do you think I am?" Savannah asked as they trotted across a dirt street holding their hems above their lace-up boots.

"Oh, I don't know. You're a very handsome woman and—"

"Don't flatter me, honey. I look near fifty, don't I?"

"Well, I . . . eh, never—"

"I'm thirty-eight years old and been a widow three times."

"You don't know that Pappy's—".

"Pepper, dear, when it happens to you, then you'll know. A wife always knows. It's how the Lord helps you get prepared."

"I don't plan on ever having to find out."

"Neither did I. Every time I say I've paid my dues. It won't happen again." Savannah pointed her gloved hand across the street.

"It looks like a crowd's still over at the Occidental. . . . Don't tell me a gunfight's still going on!"

She and Pepper scooted up behind a crowd of men who gazed at the Occidental Saloon from about fifty feet away. Savannah Divide shoved her way through.

"I've got to get to Pappy, boy! Doc Wagoner, why aren't you in there taking care of my husband?" she demanded of the tall, thin man wearing a charcoal-gray wool vest.

"Miz Savannah! Someone's still in there shooting up the place."

"Where's Deputy Andrews?" Pepper asked.

"Up there trying to talk him out."

Reaching the front of the crowd, Pepper could see Tap hunched down outside one of the tall front doors of the Occidental Saloon. The opaque glass had been shot out, and he held his cocked .44 in his right hand. Several blasts rang out from inside the saloon. She heard glass shatter. Most in the crowd cowered back, but she stood pat, straining to hear what Tap was shouting.

"Hager . . . it's me, Deputy Andrews. I'm givin' you a chance to lay down those guns and walk out of there!"

"You know where you can go, Deputy!" a deep voice boomed.

"Look, if you don't come out peaceful, I'll come in and have to kill you."

"You ain't that good, Andrews. I've got the door covered. And everyone else in here's dead or dyin'."

"I am that good, and you know it. You're drunk, Jerome. I come through that door and you won't stand a chance."

There was silence for a moment as the crowd on the street regained its courage and inched forward, scooting Pepper and Savannah ahead of them.

Another shot was fired inside, and more glass shattered.

"You might as well come in, Deputy. If I turn myself in, I'll hang. Don't reckon on winnin' either way it goes!"

"Come on, Hager. Maybe the jury will give you a life sentence." He motioned with his left hand for the crowd to stay back.

"I've been to the Territorial Prison in Laramie City once before. I didn't like it."

"It beats bein' planted in the ground. Lay your guns on the floor and walk on out of here with your hands in plain sight." Tap dropped down onto his knees and braced himself with his left hand on the rough two-by-eight cedar boardwalk.

"No good, Deputy. They'll lynch me before I ever see the judge. You remember what they did to 'Big Nose' George over in Rawlins!"

"You'll be safe in jail—I guarantee it."

Tap scrunched down trying to make sure he could not be seen from inside the building. *Does the Occidental have single or double walls? If he's close enough, a bullet could pass right through this wall.*

"But I'll still hang. I shot Pappy in the back. He's deader than a beaver hat."

Tap inched closer to the door. "You've got a point, Hager, but at least jail will give you time to settle up with the Almighty."

"Settle up? I'm headed to hades, and you know it."

"That can change."

"You goin' to preach at me or shoot me?"

"Both . . . if I have to."

Tap swung the shattered door open with the barrel of his Colt, and there were no shots fired from inside.

"What about it, Jerome?"

"I'm still ponderin' it."

"This crowd's gettin' restless. They want some action."

"I've got friends out there, Deputy. You'd better watch your backside."

"You're wastin' my time, Jerome. I've got to get back to the I-X-L and buy an iron-gray geldin' . . . so I'm just goin' to have to come in and shoot you now."

"Wait . . . I'm . . . I'm comin' out. Don't shoot me. Have I got your pledge you won't shoot me?"

"I don't want to see a gun in your hand or in your holster. Is that understood?" Tap hollered.

"Tell the others not to shoot me."

"They won't."

"I didn't hear you tell 'em!"

"Listen up," Tap called back at the crowd. "I'm takin' Hager to the jail. I don't want anyone shootin' at him!"

His eyes met Pepper's for the first time, and she could tell at a glance he had everything under control.

He was born for this job.

But so was Pappy Divide!

"Come on out, Jerome!"

"I'm feelin' poorly."

"I reckon you are."

"Don't shoot me."

Tap could hear heavy boot heels bang and spurs jingle across the saloon floor. He stood to his feet, backed up a couple of steps, and pointed the cocked revolver at the now open doorway.

A medium-sized, unshaven man with black hair and a wide-brimmed black hat hanging by a stampede string across his back slowly stepped into the light of the Cheyenne boardwalk. His hands were held straight out in front of him.

"Don't shoot me. You promised not to shoot me! I ain't got no gun in my hand . . . or in my holster."

He stepped into the street and then spun toward Tap. "'Course you didn't say nothin' about a . . ."

Sunlight flashed off the steel knife Hager pulled from his sleeve. But before he could raise the weapon, the barrel of Tap's Colt .44 creased Hager's forehead with such impact that it sounded almost like a gunshot. The gunman dropped like a burlap sack full of nails to the street.

Looking back at the crowd, Tap shouted, "Doc, get in there and see about Pappy and the others! Pepper, you and Savannah better wait out here. Eden, you and Trementen give me a hand packing Hager to jail."

"You really goin' to stand him for trial?" someone shouted. "I say we should just plug him right now and save us all some money!"

"Don't insult Pappy's memory by doin' somethin' dumb," Andrews warned.

"He don't deserve to live, and you know it, Deputy!"

"But he gets a trial. Everybody gets a trial. Come on, you two . . . give me a hand."

"I ain't touchin' him," Trementen insisted.

"No, sir, me either." Eden turned and walked away.

Most in the crowd surged into the Occidental to see how many dead bodies were scattered about, as well as to check on Pappy's condition.

"You need me to help you?" Pepper asked Tap as he hefted the unconscious man reeking of whiskey to his shoulder.

"You stick with Savannah. She'll need someone."

"Are you sure you want to be a lawman?" she questioned.

"Are you sure you want to be married to one?"

"I'm sure I want to be married to you."

Rolly Hayburn trotted ahead of Tap and opened the door to the marshal's office and jail next to the courthouse. Simp Merced leaned back in the marshal's chair with his hands folded behind his head.

"Simp, I could've used you down at the Occidental . . . Open cell 3," Andrews called out, short of breath.

"It's a waste of time. Hager don't deserve to live."

"That's what everyone keeps tellin' me. Open the cell."

Merced swung his polished black boots to the floor and strolled to the back of the jail.

"You hear who's bein' appointed actin' marshal?"

"I haven't even heard how Pappy is for sure," Tap puffed as he slumped Hager's body on the tongue-and-groove siding that served as a mattress board.

"You want to take guard duty?" he asked Merced.

"I'll do the rounds. You can play jailer."

"If you see Mayor Breshnan, send him my way. Simp, I suspect the bummers camped out down by the roundhouse will strike back. The town's crammed with drovers waitin' for spring work. Rolly, how about you finding out Pappy's condition?"

"Yep, that's what I'm goin' to do."

"If either of you see Baltimore or Carbine, tell 'em they don't get today off after all. Send them over, and we'll work out a guard detail. There's likely to be trouble over Hager."

"It's a guarantee there'll be trouble," Rolly Hayburn mumbled as he scooted out of the jail.

"Callin' Baltimore and Carbine back to work . . . I thought only the marshal could do that," Merced complained. "Are you assumin' that position?"

"I'm assumin' you, me, Baltimore, and Carbine need to earn our pay. You know it's goin' to take all of us by the time the loafers and bummers get liquored up and full of whiskey courage."

"If they go on the prod, I doubt that a dozen men can hold them back. Those drovers have been tryin' to stir up a fight for weeks. I figure they've gone off and done it this time." Merced yanked on his black hat and sauntered through the door.

Tap unlocked the gun case and pulled out another .44, which he stuck in his belt. *My heart isn't in this, Lord. Pappy was a good man . . . maybe too good.*

He glanced up to see Pepper walking up the stairs to the jail.

"Pappy's dead, Tap."

"How's Savannah?"

"She says she's doing all right. She keeps spouting Scriptures, but there's only so much one woman can take."

"How are you doin'?"

Pepper slid behind him and began to rub his neck.

"I keep thinking about what I would do if it were you lying dead in the Occidental."

"What would you do?" He swiveled around in the chair and held her soft, white hands in his rough, callused ones.

"I'd lay down and die, Tapadera Andrews."

"Well . . . it's not me. Maybe Pappy was too trusting. You don't ever turn your back on anyone in a place like the Occidental. Maybe a half-tamed town is the worst kind of all."

"What do you mean?"

"If you walk into a saloon in Deadwood or Tombstone or Bodie, you can expect to be bushwhacked from every angle. You waltz into a place in Virginia City or San Francisco, and you can pretty much count on being safe. But Cheyenne . . . it deceives you. Just when you get impressed with those big Ferguson Street houses and the fancy people at the concert at the Opera House, then some bummer wanders in from the roundhouse or a drover off the Texas trail tryin' to shoot each other and anyone who comes between them."

Pepper scooted onto his lap and slipped her arm around his neck. "You figure on getting elected marshal?"

"I don't know if I'm the right one for the job. But being a deputy sure don't pay a man much."

"We're doin' okay."

"As long as we don't eat supper at a hotel, you keep wearin' Miss Cedar's clothes, the city pays the rent, and we don't take any trips."

"Tap Andrews, don't you start feeling sorry for me. A year ago I was working at April's dance hall, hating myself and my job. I didn't have two dresses I could wear in decent company. Now I've got everything I ever wanted. How about you?"

Tap plopped his hat on the desk, crown down, and squeezed her narrow waist.

"All I ever wanted was you, darlin' . . . and that Triple Creek Ranch down in Colorado."

"Well . . . we lost that ranch, so there must be a better one on up ahead."

"Mrs. Andrews, you're a stander."

"I'm going to keep pushing until you get that ranch, Mr. Andrews!"

"I believe you, lady!" Tap brushed his chapped lips across hers. "But we can't save ranch money on a deputy's salary."

"If you'd let me get a job as cook at one of the hotels, we could save my money for the ranch."

"I don't want you to ever talk that way. You aren't ever goin' to have to work again."

"You're a stubborn man, Tap Andrews."

"And crazy about you."

She kissed his cheek and stood up. "You goin' to be home for dinner?"

"If I'm not there by two, how about you bringin' me a plate?"

"You can count on it, Mr. Lawman."

She threw her arms around him for one last hug.

"What was that for?"

"Because you weren't the one lying dead at the Occidental."

The first explosion rattled their eardrums, shattered the office windows, and slammed them both against the gun case. At the second blast, Tap rolled Pepper under the big oak table. He drew his revolver and pointed it at the door.

Pepper tried to peek out.

"Stay under there!"

"What was that? A shotgun?"

"Dynamite, more than likely."

"A lynch party?"

"Not during daylight. Stay there!"

Tap crawled across the wooden floor, trying not to cut his hands on the shattered glass. He lifted his head to the window; then he dove to the floor as two shots rang out. Bullets smashed into the back wall of the office.

"It must be Jerome's compadres comin' to break him out."

"Already?"

"Reckon they figure on stayin' ahead of the lynch mob."

He scampered on his hands and knees to the back of the office toward the jail cells.

"Where you going?" she cried out.

"To check on the prisoner. There were two explosions! Stay under the desk!"

As Tap entered the cell area, still crawling along the floor, the first thing he noticed was the narrow, iron-barred window blown out. One brick had tumbled to the floor. The room was so filled with fine red dust it was like peering through fog. He fought the urge to cough. With gun in hand, he inched closer. Hager still lay unconscious.

"Jerome?" someone outside hollered.

A hand and pistol stuck through the broken window. "Jerome . . . grab this .45. This blasted wall didn't blow. . . . Jerome?"

Tap unlocked the iron door and crept into the cell.

"Hurry up, Jerome. My arm's about to fall off, and folks are comin'!"

Tap grabbed the man's arm and hollered back at the office, "Pepper, bring me some hand irons!"

The man squeezed the trigger. A bullet shattered the floor near Tap's feet. As he jumped back, he released his grip. The arm disappeared back out the window. Tap leaped to the corner of the bunk and looked out the broken window only to see the backside of a man pushing his way through a crowd on the far side of the street.

"Tap, are you all right?" Pepper stood at the door holding a shotgun and wrist irons. "Were they trying to blow a hole in the wall?"

"I don't think they knew what they were doin'. They could have done that much damage with a stone."

Tap locked the cell behind him and took the shotgun from Pepper's hand. "Come on." He motioned with a sweeping gesture. "I need you out of here."

Out front Tap studied the crowd that had gathered.

"Tap, I don't want you to be deputy anymore. I want you to come home . . . and I want you to hold me and never let go."

"It will be okay, darlin'."

When Tap and Pepper appeared on the steps of the marshal's office, the crowd inched closer.

"Everything all right, Deputy?"

"Did they shoot Hager?"

"He didn't escape, did he?"

"You and Mrs. Andrews unhurt?"

The last speaker was Tom Breshnan, now pushing through the crowd.

"We're fine. Thanks for askin', Mayor." He shoved Pepper gently. "Go on. I'll see you later, babe."

She swept down the steps and into the throng.

"Folks, everything is fine. We had a little fireworks and lost some glass—that's all."

Pulling Tap aside, the mayor asked, "Andrews, what happened down at the Occidental?"

"Rolly Hayburn said some Black Hills loafers and bummers wandered in and started denigratin' the great state of Texas, cattle drovers, and ranchin' in general."

"In other words, looking for a fight?"

"Yep. I guess lead started flyin', and the room filled with smoke when Pappy burst in figurin' to talk them into law and order. He always figured there was a reasonable streak in every man. Well, Jerome Hager was stewed and firing at anything that moved . . . and shot Pappy in the back."

Mayor Breshnan tiptoed across the broken glass in the marshal's office to glance at the cells.

"Hager still alive?"

"Yep. I reckon he's sufferin' from a headache."

"Andrews, it's not a very Christian thing to say . . . but I surely wish Hager had died in the shootout. He's been in jail thirty minutes, and already there's chaos. Cheyenne will be in an uproar as long as he's in here. There'll be a lynch gang tonight. You know that. What are we goin' to do?"

Tap grabbed a broom and swept up the shattered glass. Slivers ground under his boot heels. He glanced over at the mayor. "You'd better appoint an acting marshal first off."

"Actually, I can only appoint a temporary acting marshal. The city council appoints an acting marshal."

"Whatever." Tap scooped up broken pieces of glass and tossed them with a tinkle and crash into an old milk bucket that served as a trash can.

"Well, Andrews, I hereby appoint you temporary acting marshal."

"I'm not the only deputy."

"You and I know Baltimore wouldn't take it. Williams is a half-breed, and Merced . . . well, he's too ambitious to make a good marshal."

"He won't like me bein' boss."

"Well, he can get by for a while."

"Mayor, I think you ought to get a glazier over here immediately and replace these windows. It would give the folks confidence that ever'thing's under control."

"But what about—"

Simp Merced burst through the front door. "Andrews, what happened? They didn't shoot Hager already, did they?"

"Who's they? Is someone goin' to try to shoot him?"

"I mean . . . you know . . . a lynch mob," Merced stammered.

"No, not yet. Some friends tried to bust him out."

A big man with a stained brown vest and gray-streaked, cropped black hair hurried into the office.

"Baltimore, scout around and see if you can find a friend of Hager's in a red shirt carryin' a walnut-handled .45. Simp, go check the south side and see if you can find out why those bummers barged into a cowboy bar and picked a fight in the first place. With a town full of drovers, that doesn't seem too smart."

"You're givin' a lot of orders," Merced complained.

"Andrews is acting as temporary marshal until our next city council meeting," Breshnan announced.

Merced glared at Tap and then ambled slowly toward the glassless front door.

"You'll need to check more than just the brass rail at DelGatto's," Tap insisted.

"Look, Andrews, I don't need you tellin' me what I can and can't do."

"Well, I'm tellin' you to get in line with Andrews," the mayor huffed. "And it's my name on your pay voucher."

"Yes . . . sir," Merced intoned in a sarcastic drawl and left the room.

"Now, Andrews, what were you saying?" the mayor pressed.

Tap glanced back toward the cells. "I don't think we can hold Hager here. I figure the only way we'll keep him safe until trial time is to move him out of town . . . say, to Denver . . . or the Territorial Prison up at Laramie City."

"Well, we can't send him out of the territory. That would be admitting we can't handle our own trouble. We'll never talk them into statehood that way," Breshnan insisted. "It's a Cheyenne problem; we have to settle it."

"Maybe we could send him to Ft. Russell; they're only three miles away," Tap suggested.

"That's still calling in the federal troops, don't you see?"

"Well," Tap drawled, "a lynchin' don't seem all that civilized either." He rubbed the stubble of a two-day beard and brushed back his mustache with his fingers. "How about that old stockade at Swan's ranch? We held those rustlers up there in February during the blizzard."

"That's over forty miles!"

"If we packed him in a freight wagon headed for the Black Hills, no one would be suspicious."

"You mean, just pirate him out of town?"

"Just you and me would know where he was."

"Perhaps I should check with the U.S. Marshal's office."

"They're chasin' renegade Arapahos up in the Big Horns."

"Well, Governor Hale's in Washington and—"

"Am I temporary acting marshal or not?"

"Yes, yes, of course. It's your decision. We'll send Hager to the stockade. Swan will probably be at the Cheyenne Club. I can talk to him there."

"If you see Baltimore or Carbine Williams, send him back, and I'll have one of 'em pull guard duty while I line up a wagon."

"How about Merced?"

"I'd just as soon leave him out of this."

"Yes, well . . . I suppose, but still . . ." Thomas Breshnan straightened his bowler and shuffled out the door.

About the time Baltimore Gomez sauntered back into the office, a short man wearing overalls showed up to repair the broken windows. By then Andrews had transferred Hager to cell #1, but he still kept him handcuffed to the bars.

"You want to see me, Tap?" Baltimore asked.

"Yeah. Guard Hager while I go do a little business."

"You reckon others will try to bust him out?"

"I can't imagine Jerome Hager havin' many friends. But I guess there's a general principle of stickin' up for each other. Anyway, I don't expect more trouble until dark."

"We goin' to move the prisoner?"

"Yep."

"Folks is sayin' you'll ship Hager over to Ft. Russell."

"Sounds like a good plan, doesn't it?"

"Yeah . . . providin' none of them decide to vigilante up and take matters into their own hands along the way. You'll be needin' me to ride with you, I suppose."

"Actually, I'll need you, Carbine, and Merced to stay here and take care of Cheyenne."

"You takin' Hager by yourself?"

"If I can make the arrangements."

Tap headed downtown on Ferguson Street. He didn't slow his pace until he was in front of the big two-story brick Union Mercantile building. Several freight wagons lined the alley. Two were being loaded at the front door.

A slightly balding man wheeled out a hand cart full of goods.

"Mr. Whipple, are any of these wagons headed up to Deadwood?"

"They're all going to Deadwood."

"Who's your best driver?"

"Fastest? Or most reliable?"

"Most reliable."

"That big, old boy with the six mules. You got something to ship north?"

"Maybe."

"I've got a full load for him," Whipple informed him.

"I'd like to talk to him."

"Be my guest."

"What's his name?"

"Lowery. Stack Lowery."

2

"Hey, you muscle-bound, pitiful excuse for a piano player, did you steal that rig, or did you decide to finally get an honest job?" Tap hollered at the tall, broad-shouldered man with thick brown hair curling out under his floppy hat. "You couldn't follow a wagon of loose hay across a forty-acre field, let alone teamster."

Two employees of Whipple and Hay scampered back inside the Mercantile. Several folks scattered across the street.

"Tapadera Andrews! Surely the fine citizens of Cheyenne are smart enough not to hire an Arizona gunslinger to wear the badge. I surely hope that Miss Pepper had enough sense to dump you for an honest man! It stifles the mind why someone hasn't pulled your picket pin by now!"

"Lowery, you can color a story redder than a Navajo blanket! If I can live through a plate of those slimy eggs of yours, I figure I'm goin' to live forever!"

"You insultin' my eggs?" the big man growled.

"I am. Those eggs would make a hen blush with embarrassment. In fact, it's only my Christian gentility that prevents me from properly describin' them."

"Your breathin' days are over, Andrews. Ain't no man alive who can insult my cookin' and live! Why, I'll kick you so far it'll take a bloodhound six weeks just to find your smell!"

A crowd began to grow on the far side of the street. Suddenly the tall man's menacing glare turned into a full-toothed grin. He threw his arm around Tap's shoulder, and his massive hand gripped Tap's with obvious delight. As both men laughed, the boardwalk refilled with people, and the white-aproned loaders for Whipple and Hay sheepishly scooted back out to their work.

"How you been, Stack? We haven't seen or heard from you since three days after the weddin'. We've been worried sick about you."

"You're treatin' my Pepper girl good, ain't ya?"

"We're doin' great, Stack—starvin' to death on deputy's wages, but we're doin' great. How about you? What's with this freight wagon? Where're the girls? Don't tell me they all grew up and left home."

They stepped over near the wall of the building and stood under one of the tall, white limestone-block arches.

"Seems funny, don't it? Me not working the houses and lookin' after a string of dance-hall girls?"

"Last we heard, you, Selena, Paula, and Danni Mae were goin' to Laramie City. Then when we lost the ranch, we came by that way, and no one had ever seen you."

"Sure am sorry about the ranch, Tap. I guess Fightin' Ed Casey has a lot of pull. It's a wonder he let you get hired here in Cheyenne."

"Fightin' Ed has friends and enemies. I guess it was his enemies that hired me. Besides, he doesn't come into Cheyenne all that much."

Stack Lowery swung up in the driver's seat of his wagon. "Let me get this rig back into the loadin' dock, and I'll tell you what happened." He drove the team up the alley to the front of Whipple and Hay's. Parallel to the dock, he swung the team out across the street, which turned the wagon perpendicular to the dock.

He's right. It does seem strange for Stack not to have a passel of girls to look after.

The roadway was still wet enough to keep the dust down. A west wind stirred. The wide dirt street held only a little traffic as Stack pulled out the tailgate from the wagon and stepped over to where Tap was waiting. Both men watched the Deadwood Stagecoach rumble north.

Stack shoved his hat to the back of his head. "When we got to Laramie City, a letter was waitin' for us from April. She had already gone into partnership in a hurdy-gurdy in Denver and wanted us all to come down. Well, when we got there, we found out the place she bought into was the Pearly Gate. Remember that wild dive on the edge of town?"

"Rena used to own part of that. It's a tough crowd."

"That's the one. The gents ain't got no better. Anyway . . . by the time we get down there, Danni Mac and Wiley decided to get married, move to west Texas, and take up the plow."

"No foolin'? Danni Mae and Wiley? Homesteadin'? Wait 'til I tell Pepper. She said it would happen like that."

"And April's partner in the business turned out to be Silky Peterson."

"The one with all the gold mines?"

"Yep. He takes one look at Selena and puts her up in a nice hotel apartment."

"That just leaves Paula to work the Pearly Gate."

"She worked there two days, took her money, and bought a ticket to Omaha. Ain't heard from her since."

"How about you?"

"I didn't hire on."

"You gettin' out of the dance-hall business?"

"You and me findin' little Rocky out there all froze up—I got to where I . . . it's just when I think about them girls."

Stack turned away. "Girls shouldn't work them houses, Tap. It just tears 'em down. That ain't right," he mumbled, brushing his sleeve across his face.

"So you became a teamster?"

"You remember my baby sister in Denver?"

"Yeah. How is she doin'?"

Stack's eyes brightened. "Very well, thank you. Her husband freights for this outfit and landed me a job. I've spent a couple months on some short runs in the Black Hills. But the real money is on these long hauls."

"You've got to stop by and say hello to Pepper. She'll kill me if I don't ask you for supper."

"You livin' here in town?"

"Over on East 17th."

"I'll surely roll by before I head out, but I can't do more than greet her. Got a tight schedule. They pay you a bonus if you get there early. Pretty good money, Tap. You might consider joinin' up. Ain't many Sioux up there anymore, you know."

"I've got a job." He looked up to see a pencil-thin man wearing a dark red shirt lope his paint horse toward the tracks. "Do you know that hombre's name?" he asked Stack.

"I don't know anybody in Cheyenne, Tap. Why?"

"Oh . . . I'm searchin' for some man in a red shirt. He blew up some windows at the jail. Look, Stack, I've got to take a prisoner out of town before he gets himself lynched. You got room for two of us to ride along this afternoon?"

"A freight wagon is mighty slow transportation."

"I just need to get him well out of town on the sly. After that, we'll mount up and be on our own."

"You got to hide him in the goods? Or do we sit him right up here on the bench?"

"The bench is all right as long as we head north and don't look back. Nobody in town will be watchin' a Deadwood freighter."

"What time you want me at the jail?" Stack asked.

"Not the jail. They're all eyeglassin' the jail. I'll have you pull back of the courthouse where they unload goods. I'll have him around there. When you headin' out?"

"Two o'clock. Who's the prisoner?"

Andrews lowered his voice and stepped closer to Lowery. "Jerome Hager, but this is between you and me."

"Hager? The one who killed the marshal?"

"You heard about it?"

"I heard some fool deputy bluffed Hager out of the Occidental and coldcocked him without havin' to fire a shot. I should have figured it was you. 'Course, most folks I talked to wished you had plugged him."

"So I hear. I'll let Pepper know you're comin' by. It's on 17th just past Evans. North side of the street. It's an unpainted cottage with blue curtains."

"You still got that piano?"

"Yep, but it's almost as big as the whole house."

"Either of you learn how to play it yet?"

"Nope."

"I'll get a day off on the return. I'll come by and bang you out a tune or two just for old times' sake. Then you two will have to let me buy you a fine hotel supper."

"That's what I like—rich friends!"

Tap hired Rolly Hayburn to lead Brownie and Onespot out past the north park. Then he double-checked the details with Mayor Breshnan at his hotel office. After that he walked back to the jail and made sure all was secure with Baltimore. It was past noon when he made it home for dinner.

"You'll never guess who I ran into at Whipple and Hay's," he announced as he burst through the door.

"And you'll never guess who we got a letter from."

"Stack Lowery!" Tap declared.

"Wade Eagleman!" she reported.

"Stack's freightin' on the Deadwood."

"Wade and Rena are in Arizona."

Tap hung his hat on a peg. "He's completely out of the dance-hall business."

Pepper wiped her hands on her apron. "Wade says they got the charges against you dropped!"

"Did you know that Danni Mae and Wiley got married and moved to Texas?" He unbuttoned his sleeves and began to roll them up his arm.

"Tap, are you listening to me?"

"Huh? Yeah . . . what?"

"Are you listening to me?"

"Eh . . . yeah!" Tap gazed into her green eyes. "Did you say Wade got me off? What about the escape charge?"

"Danni Mae and Wiley got married?" she squealed.

"I told you that old Comanche, Wade, could do it! Didn't I tell you?"

"What about Paula?" Pepper quizzed. "And Selena? Where are they?"

"Rena didn't have to go to jail, did she?"

She shook her head. "I just can't believe Stack's not playin' piano and bouncin' drunks."

Tap pointed his finger at her. "That Wade's a mighty good man."

"Eh . . . what?"

Tap's eyes danced. "I said he's a good man."

"Yes." Pepper relaxed. "Stack's one of the most decent, best-hearted men I ever met in my whole life."

"Stack? Are we talkin' about Stack?"

"Tapadera Andrews, let's take this conversation down one trail at a time. This is a letter from Wade. The McCurleys got it at the hotel, and they sent it on up to us. You read it, and then you'll know what I'm talking about."

When he finished reading the letter, Pepper served up more potatoes and gravy and then slipped onto the bench beside him. As they ate, he retold her everything he heard from Lowery.

"How long will you be gone up at Swan's stockade?" she finally asked.

"Two days . . . maybe three if a storm blows in."

"Do you expect trouble?"

"If I can get Hager to the stockade unnoticed, there'll be no trouble at all."

"What about on the way up there?"

"I don't think they'll figure it out. Anyway, it's worth a chance. If there has to be trouble, I'd rather it didn't blow up in town. A group of those roundhouse bummers have been hanging out at DelGatto's gaming house. They don't act like they're in any hurry to get up to the diggin's. They seem mighty resolved to stir up a fight with the cowboys who are waitin' to pull out with the roundup wagons. Hager or some drover plugged a couple bummers before he shot Pappy. I figure they'll use this to get a big battle ragin'. All sorts of townsfolk can get hurt in somethin' like that."

Wrinkles beyond her years showed around Pepper's eyes. "But you can only do so much."

"I will not let anyone take a prisoner out of my jail unlawfully— no matter how guilty the man is. We've got to preserve decency and order for the times when it will be an innocent man in there."

Pepper smiled, shook her head at him, and tried to laugh.

Tap's stern expression melted into a stare. "What's the matter? What'd I say?"

"Your jail? You take everything so personal. You seem to be able to take any situation you're in and make it a turning point in the history of mankind."

He tensed up and blushed. Then he flashed a relaxed smile. "I guess I do, don't I?"

"Yes, you do." She slipped her fingers into his. "But I like it. It makes every day seem important. I think that's maybe the way the Lord intended it."

Tap gave her a hug, then stood, and grabbed his gray wide-brimmed hat. "Darlin', sometimes I wonder if I'm right for this job. I don't have a lot of patience with some of 'em."

"You're a good deputy."

"Well, I surely had to hold myself back from shootin' Hager on sight myself." He slipped his arm around her shoulder. "You goin' to be all right for a few days, darlin'?"

"I'll be lonesome and worried. But Savannah did ask me to spend some time with her. I'll probably just camp over there during the daytime."

"That's good. She'll keep you occupied, that's for sure."

"But I can only spend so much time with her before I start buyin' dresses and jewelry," she teased.

"She won't be shoppin', will she? She'll be wearin' black."

"Yes, but a very stylish, fashionable black."

Tap stared at Pepper's green eyes and caressed her long, curly blonde hair. "Even in her prime, she couldn't have been as handsome as you, Mrs. Andrews."

"In her prime? Don't you ever let Savannah know she's not in her prime."

"You think she wouldn't handle that too well?"

"I think," Pepper flashed, "that I would wind up a widow too."

The window had been completely replaced by the time Tap got back to the jail. Baltimore sat at the marshal's desk feasting on a plate of chops and cabbage. His ten-year-old daughter sat across the room holding a large empty basket in her lap, watching him eat.

"I had Angelita bring my dinner."

Tap tipped his hat at the scrubbed-clean young girl in the faded green dress. "You look quite pretty today, Miss Angelita."

"And you look very handsome, Mr. Andrews." She grinned and then looked down at her worn black lace-up shoes.

Tap glanced back at Baltimore's wide smile. "How about the prisoner? Did you feed him?"

"I tried to, but I don't think he ate much. I figure maybe he's too tuckered out to eat."

"Tuckered out?"

"Yep. He spent nearly an hour screamin', yellin', and cussin' the day of your birth."

"Then Hager's awake?"

"Says he has a terrible headache and doesn't remember anything about the shootin'. Wants to know if it's legal to hang a man who doesn't recall what he did."

"How did he remember we wanted to hang him?"

"Say . . . I never thought of that!"

"Listen, Baltimore, I'm takin' Hager with me for a few days until things cool off. You, Carbine, and Merced will have to look after things until I get back."

"So you're not takin' him to Ft. Russell?"

"Nope." Tap glanced over at Angelita. "I was thinkin' about buryin' him in a prairie dog hole." He winked at her.

"Obviously, Mr. Andrews does not want me to hear where he's taking the man who viciously murdered Pappy," she pouted. "In that case I'll just go home and come back for the dishes later, no matter how much burden and extra work that brings into my already toilsome life."

"You're not mad at me, are you? I'd be miserable for three days if you were," Tap teased.

Her dark brown eyes sparkled. She brushed her black hair over her shoulder. "So you're goin' to be gone three days? In that length of time you could take him to Denver or Rawlins or Ft. Laramie, or even Salt Lake City if you rode the train."

Tap waved his hands at her. "Out of here. Go on . . . shoo. We've got marshalin' to do."

"You have got to stop bullying young ladies!" she lectured.

"And you, young lady, have got to stop selling worthless mining stock to every greenhorn who gets off the train."

"How did I know the stocks were worthless? I've never been to the Black Hills. Besides, I'm a child."

"Only in size."

"Very well, I'll go. . . . Poor Mrs. Andrews. I really don't know how she puts up with the likes of you day after day!"

"Angelita!" Baltimore scolded. "You shouldn't talk about Tap like that."

"Oh, Papa, Mr. Andrews knows I'm teasing him. We understand each other. He and I are very much alike, you know." She bounded out the door and down the steps.

"She is a very—eh, ambitious girl," Baltimore apologized. "I think she will probably own a gold mine before she's twenty-five."

Tap smiled. "I figure she'll own one before she's sixteen. Listen, I'm taking Jerome back to the loading docks. I'm goin' to slip him out of town in a freight wagon. No reason to let the drovers or the bummers know which way I'm taking him."

"You need me to ride guard with you up to Swan's stockade?"

"How did you know?"

Baltimore dropped his fork and scratched behind his ear. "Well . . . dad gum it, Tap, Parker down at the telegraph office mentioned that the mayor had some hush business with Swan over at the Cheyenne Club, and I, eh, guess I figured it out. But I didn't tell nobody. Shoot, I didn't even tell Angelita!"

If Baltimore figured it out, everyone in town knows!

Simp Merced pushed his way into the office and looked startled to see Tap. "Andrews! It's spreadin' around town that you're headed out of town with the prisoner in a freight wagon. There's talk of a lynchin' down across the tracks. They don't aim to let you get him to Swan's."

"Now how do you suppose they know what I'm doin'?"

"Strappler down at DelGatto's said it was all over town."

"Why don't I just parade Hager up and down the streets like bait? Sooner or later someone will shoot him," Tap fumed.

"Or you," Baltimore added. "There's drovers in this town that think Hager was juiced up and suckered into a gunfight."

"This town is crammed with drovers on the prod," Merced put in. "The bummers are just tryin' to keep from gettin' shot."

Baltimore Gomez shrugged and turned to Tap. "What are you goin' to do now?"

Andrews paced the office. He pulled a .44 bullet from his belt and twisted it in his fingers as he stared back through the small window in the door that led to the cells. Then he spun on his heels and faced the other two deputies.

"Simp, you go back to the row and keep watch over the bummers. If you can stall them a while, it will give me some time."

"I ain't goin' to try to back down a whole legion of them," Merced insisted. "I don't intend to put my life on the line for the likes of Jerome Hager."

"No, I don't want you to do anything that would jeopardize your safety," Tap sneered. "After all, lawmen shouldn't have to risk gettin' shot, should they?"

Simp moved his right hand on the pearl handle of his revolver and looked intently at Andrews. Finally he turned and left the office.

"I thought maybe he was goin' to draw on you."

"Simp wouldn't draw on anyone face to face. But I probably shouldn't have pressed him like that. I'm not sure gunmen always make good lawmen." Tap took a deep breath. "Baltimore, I need you to work twenty-four hours straight. Can you do that?"

"Long as I get my meals." He grinned. "What are you goin' to do?"

"This time I tell no one. Stack Lowery is supposed to bring around a freight wagon to the loading dock behind the courthouse in about half an hour. Keep an eye out for him. Tell him we're goin' ahead with the plan."

"What plan?"

"I haven't quite decided yet."

Tap burst out the door and strode down the street. On 16th he stopped to rent Chang Lee's white sideboard delivery van. Then he swung by the house. Pepper, dressed in a long brown dress and matching hat, her cape across her shoulders and a satchel in her hand, was just leaving the house.

"You movin' out?" he teased.

"Tap, what are you doin' still in town? Savannah asked me to stay at her place while you're gone. So I gathered up a few things. Is that all right?"

"I was about to suggest the very same thing."

"You were?"

"This thing of protectin' a prisoner is snowballin', darlin'. I've changed plans about where to take Hager."

"Where will you keep him?"

"Here at our house."

"Are you serious?"

"Yep. Don't tell anyone—especially Savannah."

"How could I? I don't know what's going on. But don't worry. I'm good at keepin' secrets. Did you know I once convinced this driftin' Arizona gunslinger that I was a proper lady from back east?"

"You mean some dumb guy actually fell for that?"

"Like a rock in a cistern." She winked. "Shall I stay there until you tell me it's safe to come home?"

"Yep."

"Do you know what you're doing?"

"Nope."

"Well, at least I'm glad you're not going out of town."

"I didn't say that."

Pepper stared. "I'm totally confused."

"Good. I'll check with you tomorrow." He gave her a squeeze and returned to the laundry van.

"I'm not even goin' to ask what you're doing with Chang Lee's wagon," she called out.

He tipped his hat at her and drove off toward the jail. The few scattered clouds of early morning had drifted west, and the breeze was slightly cool. The air tasted like springtime. Tap thought of green grass on hillsides, creeks running high with snowmelt, and calves playing under the watchful eyes of their mothers.

Lord, Pepper's right. There's got to be a ranch for us out there somewhere. Someplace where life is slower . . . and safer than in Cheyenne.

He pulled the laundry wagon up right in front of the courthouse. Hiking back to the jail, he packed two empty six-foot-long canvas laundry bags under his arm. His eyes surveyed each person on the sidewalk, wondering which were Hager's friends and which were his enemies.

Baltimore stood looking out the newly replaced window as Tap came up the stairs.

"You goin' into business with the Chinese?" he prodded.

"Only for an hour. Help me get Hager into this laundry bag."

"Are you plum crazy?"

"Probably. But I'm goin' to do it anyway."

Jerome Hager was still chained to the bars of his cell. "You've got to take these irons off my hands! It ain't comfortable," he protested.

"I'm not going to take those off you, but I aim to give you a different view."

"You can't hang me until I see a judge. You promised I'd be safe and get me a trial. I got your warranty on that."

Andrews unlocked the irons and refastened them behind Hager's back. "Jerome, I'm workin' awful hard to keep you alive. But if you want to survive the night, you'll just have to crawl into the laundry sack and keep real quiet. I've got to sneak you out of town."

"I ain't goin' to crawl into no sack!"

"Then I reckon I'll just have to coldcock you again. Hope you don't take it personal." Tap raised his Colt .44 above Hager's head.

"Wait! Wait a minute! I don't need another blue lump on my skull. I'm still throbbin' from last time. Are you sure you know what you're doin'?" He scrunched down as Baltimore pulled the canvas bag over him.

"Don't worry. I do know what I'm doin'. 'Course, I don't know if it will work."

"Andrews! You . . ."

"Now, Jerome, don't you go and blaspheme. I need you to keep real still. If we can make folks believe you're a bundle of laundry, you might live to see another day.

"Baltimore, in about ten minutes Stack will pull up behind the courthouse. I'm going to load that other sack into his rig and ride shotgun north. As far as anyone is concerned, Hager is on that freight wagon.

"Those who are interested will sneak along watching us leave town. About fifteen minutes after we leave, no one will be watching the jail anymore. I want you to tote Hager out in the sack and toss him into the laundry van. Then drive over to my house. Park the rig in the alley. Take Hager to the back room and lock him to the brass bed. Chang Lee will pick the van up in an hour or so."

"We're goin' to keep him in your house?"

"Yep. Nobody's goin' to look for him there. Guard him just like he was in jail. Pepper's gone, so you'll have the place to yourself. Help yourself to some grub and see that Jerome gets fed. I need you to guard him until I show up to relieve you. It might be the middle of the night or mornin' before I get back. If nobody follows me out of town, I'll circle back."

"Well, I'll be! You're goin' to bait them into followin' you."

"I surely hope to find out exactly who's tryin' to bust Hager out and maybe who's trying to hang him. Maybe I can get to the core of this feud."

Baltimore rubbed the stubble of his week-old beard. "Andrews, I never knowed anyone who liked being shot at more than you."

When Stack rolled up behind the Laramie County Courthouse, Tap waited with a six-foot laundry bag full of jail blankets and bricks. He struggled and hoisted it onto the top of the freight wagon.

"How did you get him in there?" Stack asked as he slapped the reins of the six-up team of mules and pulled back into the street. "Hager looks as lifeless as a sack of rocks."

Tap grinned. "Actually, there's just jail blankets and bricks in there. I'm hopin' the boys that come after us don't figure that out too soon."

Stack whistled. "So you're not takin' Hager to Swan's stockade?"

"Nope. But everybody in town thinks I am."

"So we ride out there and take the potshots?"

"Sort of."

"Where's Hager? Back at the jail?"

"Nope. I moved him to safe quarters."

"In Cheyenne?"

"Trust me."

"Tap, are you sure that *hombre malo* is worth all this trouble?"

"That's what everyone keeps askin'."

They rumbled several blocks listening only to mules' hooves and squeaking axles. Tap cradled his rifle across his knees and surveyed the street.

"Well, what's the plan, Mr. Arizona gunslinger? You reckon they're followin' us already?"

"Maybe." Tap pulled off his hat and scratched his head. His hair felt oily, dirty. "But they won't try anything until we're out of the city."

"I don't know about that. Looks like some old boy holdin' horses up there by the park." Stack pointed up the road a quarter mile. "Could be a couple ambushers."

"That's Rolly Hayburn. He's got Brownie and Onespot."

A few minutes later Stack stopped the wagon next to the horses.

"Thanks for bringin' my ponies, partner. Be sure you don't tell anyone what I'm doin'. Here's four bits for your efforts."

Rolly slipped off Brownie and scurried back toward town.

"Can you trust him to keep quiet?"

"He's a good man . . . as long as he stays sober."

"Does he drink much?"

"Only when he has money."

"You're really beggin' for it, Andrews."

"Yeah. Aren't you glad you agreed to this?"

Tap tied the horses to the back of the wagon. Soon he and Stack rolled the wagon north on the Ft. Russell to Ft. Laramie road.

"Which one you figure will show up first—Hager's drover friends or the bummers out to lynch him?"

"I'm guessin' his friends. The lynchin' crowd likes to work in the dark. Besides, most of them are too poor to own horses. I figure that might thin down their ranks. Those drovers know they better do somethin' quick before Hager ends up bein' tree trimmin'."

"Where do you reckon they'll be waitin'?"

"I figure it's too open 'til we cross the Salt Lake Road and Lodgepole Creek."

"Maybe in those hills before Carey's place?"

"Yeah. That would be as good a spot as any. But it's quite a ways down the trail."

"We goin' to wait until they shoot at us?"

"As long as we stay near that laundry sack, I figure his friends won't do much shootin'."

Clouds congregated against the Laramie Mountains to the west, but the sky remained blue above them. The temperature dropped as the afternoon progressed. Tap and Stack talked about dance halls . . . mutual friends . . . good race horses . . . the benefits of married life . . . and the money to be made in the freighting business. Mostly they watched every rock, boulder, and coulee for any signs of ambush.

The sun inched down into the cloudy western sky, and all they had spotted were hundreds of pronghorns and a few slinking coyotes.

"Where do you usually camp for the night?" Tap asked.

"Up near Swan's headquarters."

"At Chugwater?"

"Yeah. Look up there!" Stack Lowery pointed to the large boulders north of them. "That pass looks like a good place to jump someone."

"Pull up and rest the horses."

"What?"

"Let's park it right up there in the rocks and give 'em a good chance."

"Dad gum it, Tap, we don't have to wear 'Shoot Me' signs on our hats."

"Come on, Stack. It beats the boring life of a teamster, doesn't it?"

The big man slid a shotgun from under the seat and broke it open to check the chambers. He rubbed the road dust off his face

with the red bandanna that hung around his neck, and then he
roared, "Jist like bacon in the pan, boys. Come and get it!"

Racing up the hill, Stack drove the wagon to the east side of the
road, slipped to the ground, and checked the rigging on the mules.
He carried the shotgun in his left hand and kept one eye on the
tall boulders on the west side of the road. Several scrub cedars and
piñon pines struggled for existence among the rocks and baked
red ground.

"Well, boss man, what are we goin' to do?" Stack mumbled
beneath his breath. "Wait for one of us to get shot?" He turned
to see that Tap had his pistol pointed at the sack full of jail blankets and bricks.

"How about gettin' me a ladle of water from the barrel?" Tap
asked.

"You bust a leg or somethin'?"

"I've got to stay up here and guard the prisoner," Tap hollered
in a loud voice.

"Eh . . . yeah . . . right." Stack pried off the barrel lid, scooped
with the wooden ladle, and handed it, brimming with water, up
to Tap.

"This is mighty silly if there ain't no one watchin' us!" Stack
heckled.

"I was thinkin' the same thing."

Still mumbling in a low tone, Stack swung back up on the
driver's seat of the wagon. "How long are we goin' to stay here?"

"Well, you guard the prisoner, and I'll go back and check on
my ponies."

"You mean I got to hold a gun on a sack of blankets and
bricks?"

"Yeah, but be careful, Lowery. Don't let him get the drop on
you!"

Stack took a deep breath and spoke loudly, "Well, Hager,
you're in a fine fix. Back in town most folks want to hang you,
and out here . . . out here you're hogtied and traveling with that
madman, Tap Andrews. You better mind your p's and q's, you
hear? That Andrews is known to just haul off and gut-shoot a
man for lookin' cross-eyed at him. Why, you got about as much

chance escapin' as an Easter egg in an orphanage. Jist between you and me, you'd have a better gamble with a lynch mob than Mr. Tapadera Andrews."

Faking a loud whisper, Stack continued talking to the stuffed laundry bag. "I hear that down in Arizony he'd jist go on a tear and shoot ever'one in the room. Yes, sir, it makes ol' Billy Bonney look like a choirboy. If I was you, I'd lay real still and be as quiet as a sick cow in a snowbank. That's the way. . . . You jist lay right there and pray no one tries to spring you. Tap will kill you for sure if they come a shootin'."

Tap pulled himself back into the wagon.

"I think that's enough," Tap mumbled. "You really got into this. I guess there's no one here."

"I'm surely glad. This is gettin' embarrassin'. Can we go on? I can make Swan's before dark."

"Yeah, go ahead, but take it slow. We aren't going to the stockade. We'll stop this side of the headquarters."

"You aim to give plenty of chances?"

"Yep."

For the next thirty minutes neither spoke. Tap listened to the squeaking wheels and groan of the wagon. The cloud cover was still broken enough that they rumbled into the sunlight, and Tap felt his duck canvas coat warm up. His '73 Winchester across his lap, pointed at the laundry sack, Tap closed his eyes. His chin began to drop to his chest.

I need to get more sleep . . . but with Pappy gone, I suppose we'll all have longer hours.

A stiff jolt woke him. The wagon wheel had dropped into a rut. Tap sat straight up.

"What are we doin' out here? Where's the road?"

"Oh, there looked like a landslide up ahead, so I pulled out here to avoid havin' to clean the trail. You can crawl back into that laundry sack if you want to sleep."

"Landslide? Where?"

Stack pointed his gloved right hand straight to the west. "Right up there on the other side of them boulders."

"Oh . . . no!" Tap moaned. "That was probably their ambush! We ought to be over there!"

"Dad blame it, Andrews, that's the first time I ever got raked for avoidin' a trap."

"Can't we pull back over there?"

"Tap, this trip is stranger than one of them Original Melodrama's down at Tivoli Hall."

"Pull over in that draw down there!"

"You aimin' to feed the laundry sack, or what?"

"We're goin' to camp there for the night."

"Ain't nobody dumb enough to camp out in the open plains like this," Stack argued.

"Look, if we don't snag 'em by the time the moon's out, you can roll on up to Swan's ranch, and I'll ride back to town."

"The way them clouds is moundin' up against the Laramies, there ain't goin' to be no moon."

Stack dropped off into the draw and unhitched his team. "Little Bear Crick's runnin' enough water for thirsty mules. How about your ponies?"

"Yeah, but I'm goin' to leave the saddles cinched in case I have to light out in a hurry."

"Do you really want to make camp here?"

"Let's at least get a fire goin'."

"A smoky one, I reckon. Did you ever think about what we'll do if four hundred Sioux warriors come ridin' over that hill?"

"Yeah . . . pray a lot."

The mule team was staked by the creek that ran about four feet wide and half a foot deep. There was very little vegetation near it. Tap figured it was dry most of the year.

"Just exactly what are we plannin' on buildin' a fire out of? There ain't even many buffalo chips out here," Stack complained.

"Scratch around up the draw. Maybe you'll run across some sage. I'll check downstream."

"Who's going to guard the 'prisoner'?"

Tap ran his eyes swiftly around the horizon. "I've got him leg-

ironed to that box of dynamite." Tap spoke loudly and dramati-
cally. "If he tries to climb down, I'll shoot that box and blow him
to kingdom come."

Stack's grin seemed wider than his ears. He shook his head and
wandered up the creek.

Tap had a pitifully small, dry sage fire smoking and popping
within a few minutes. He glanced around for Stack.

*Where did that piano man go? Surely he didn't hike up to those
cottonwoods. We don't need that much fire.*

The faint scrape of boot heels on rocks caused him to swing up
into the wagon. He pointed the '73 Winchester at the laundry bag.
Within seconds Stack walked slowly into the clearing, his hands
above his head. Behind him strutted two men, one of whom wore
a red shirt. The other man was heavyset and looked like a
Mexican or Indian. They both held guns on Lowery.

"Well, boys, what a surprise!"

"We want Hager," the one in the red shirt demanded.

"You come any closer, and old Jerome here gets his head
blowed off."

"You cut him out of that sack. We saw you load him up out
behind the courthouse."

"You boys don't miss nothin', do ya?"

"Look, we'll shoot this teamster if you don't let him loose. So
let's just trade straight across."

"How dumb do you think I am?"

"You ain't too smart, Deputy, to camp out here!" the dark-
skinned one taunted.

"I told Stack we should've stopped up by that rock slide." Tap
tried to hold back a grin.

"Primo, this deputy is even stupider than you said. We was
waitin' up there. You didn't have a chance," the skinny man said
laughing. "Now let Jerome out."

"You boys sure enough got the drop on us."

"It was Petey's plan," Primo boasted.

Tap waved toward the men. "Well, how about one of you
comin' over here and helpin' me. He's mighty heavy."

Petey walked over to the wagon, his gun pointed at Andrews. The one called Primo guarded Stack.

"Well, you can't let him down one-handed!" Tap insisted. "Stick that hog-leg back in your holster."

"Keep that big one covered, Primo," Petey called. He shoved his gun into his holster and reached up to the canvas laundry sack.

Tap glanced over at Stack and nodded his head slightly. Then he looked back down at Petey.

"You know what, Petey?" Tap said. "Jerome just isn't worth all this trouble."

"What do ya mean?"

"Well, if he goes ridin' off with you, I'll just have to chase you down. I could waste a whole day before I found you and shot you. On the other hand, if I take him on up the road, I'll just have to go bring him back for trial. Either way it's a whole passel of trouble. And what for? Everyone knows he will hang."

Tap stared at the laundry bag. "Sorry, Jerome, but you're just more trouble than you're worth!" He squeezed the trigger and blasted a small, round hole in the laundry bag.

"Is he still movin'?" Tap fired another shot into the bag.

Petey's mouth dropped open.

Primo stared at the wagon.

Tap crashed the rifle barrel into Petey's head just above the ear.

Stack dropped Primo with an elbow into the Adam's apple and a left cross that lifted the gunman off the ground.

"Thank you, Mr. Lowery."

"You're welcome, Mr. Andrews. Now can I hitch my team back up and get on the trail?"

"Go on. I'll tie up these boys and see if I can find their horses."

"I thought they were goin' to faint dead away when you blasted that sack."

By the time Petey and Primo revived, Tap had them tied up and sitting on the ground next to what was left of the fire. He lashed the sack of blankets and bricks onto Onespot's back and tied Primo's and Petey's horses in a string behind Onespot.

Stack had hitched his team and was perched in the wagon. "You sure you want me to go on?"

"Get on up to the Black Hills and make that big money! I'll take these two back to town."

"What about that lynch mob? You surmise they're on the trail? It'll be dark soon."

"I reckon they're on their way. But they'll stay on the road. I won't. There didn't look to be a one in that DelGatto crowd that could read sign."

"Still, if they find you, you'll have to take 'em all on by yourself."

"I'm hopin' they'll follow your wagon. When they catch up to you, just tell them I ran into a little trouble and decided to take Hager someplace else."

"Well, good luck, amigo. Take care of that yellow-haired girl, Andrews. You ever treat her bad, I'll come after you like a bear with his toes stepped on."

"Yep. I imagine you would."

Stack slapped the reins and drove the wagon up the draw back toward the road. Tap helped Petey and Primo up on their mounts. He led them straight back to the rock slide on the road and turned south toward Cheyenne. Sullen, both men refused to talk until just after the sun went down.

"I can't believe you up and shot Jerome just like that. A bound man and all. It ain't   it ain't Christian. No, sir. It's against the law!" Primo groused.

"Yeah," Petey added. "What if that lynch party does come ridin' along? What are you goin' to tell 'em now that you killed Jerome?"

"If they really insist on hangin' someone, I'll let them hang you two."

"That ain't funny, Deputy! That ain't one bit funny!"

3

The sun slipped behind the western mountains, but the cloud cover prevented any sight of a sunset. Instead, Tap watched a gray evening grow even drearier as the clouds hung low and dark. Rather than face the travelers on the Ft. Russell to Ft. Laramie road, he led his two prisoners further east, then turned south toward Cheyenne, blazing a new trail across the brown-grass prairie. The air cooled off, announcing the real possibility of cold rain or snow before morning.

Plans sure do seem easier when I'm thinkin' 'em up. We can't stop for a fire; we can't stop to eat . . . and somewhere over on that road there's probably a half-drunk gang of idiots lookin' for a lynchin'. Maybe Stack's right. Maybe I should try freightin'. Lord, I'm not all that sure this deputy job brings out the best in me.

The corduroy collar of his ducking coat chilled the back of his neck. He reached into his saddlebag for a bandanna that he knew wasn't there.

Lord, freightin' would bore me to tears.

But with Pappy gone, maybe it's time to leave Cheyenne. You know, after it all settles down. When they get themselves a new marshal. Whenever Hager gets his due. Justice, Lord. Hager ought to get exactly what he deserves.

Maybe there's something for me to do that Pepper won't worry so much about. Lord, she deserves a settled life—on a ranch . . . on a ranch like the Triple Creek.

I don't know why we couldn't have kept it. It's all I ever wanted, Lord. You know I never pestered You for much. Just that ranch . . . and Pepper . . . and to get out of the Arizona Territorial Prison and . . .

"Andrews, we ain't goin' to ride all the way back to town without stoppin' for a fire, are we?"

"Petey, if you wanted to be comfortable, you should have stayed at the Drovers' Cafe. We aren't stoppin'!"

"It's startin' to rain," Primo complained. "I can't even screw down my hat and turn up my collar with my hands tied behind my back."

"You two aren't goin' to melt in the rain."

"I think I'm gettin' a touch of pneumonia, Deputy. It ain't goin' to do it no good bein' out here all night."

Tap reined up on Brownie and turned back to the two bound gunmen.

"Boys, I can just plug ya and stuff you in a laundry sack like old Jerome. Or you can sit here in the storm like I am and get a little cold and wet. Now what's it goin' to be?"

"I just can't believe you shot Jerome while he was sacked!" Petey complained. "It was those bummers that started the gunplay. If the marshal would have stayed out of it, we could have settled it ourselves."

"That might be, but Hager shot Pappy Divide point-blank in the back and killed him dead. Why should Hager get treated better than Pappy?"

"Jerome was probably jist scared Pappy was on to him."

Tap kept Brownie moving forward, but he turned and placed his hand on Brownie's rump so he could look back at Primo and Petey, still barely visible in the evening shadows. "What do you mean, on to him?"

"Jerome had been avoidin' lawmen like they was a swamp ever since that trouble in Dodge City."

"What trouble was that?"

"You ain't heard?" Primo sounded surprised.

"No, I don't reckon I have, but I doubt if it would astonish me."

"Don't tell him nothin', Primo."

"Hager's dead now. It surely don't matter none. Anyway, two faro dealers in Dodge turned up dead in the alley, and Jerome was the last person to play at each layout, so some of 'em surmised he shot them both."

"In the back, I presume," Tap commented.

"That's what they say, but Jerome said he didn't remember doing it. Anyway, we barely got him out of town before they tried to lynch him in Dodge."

"If I were you, I'd find better friends."

"He's a top hand when he's sober."

"Of course," Petey added, "he ain't ever sober when he's in town."

"It's cold, Andrews," Primo whined. "We know a place up in the chaparral that's protected from the wind. We could build a fire and . . ."

Tap turned back to the south and tugged Onespot's lead rope, which automatically pulled the other two horses as well.

"We aren't stoppin', boys, so quit bellyachin'. You're goin' to Cheyenne and stand charges for tryin' to blow a hole in the side of the jail, bustin' out the front windows, and pullin' a gun on me and Stack."

The rain streamed down heavily for almost an hour. The ground turned slick, and it grew so dark Tap could no longer tell if he was heading toward Cheyenne or away from it. Finally, he led them back to the main road. A faint path could be seen in the menacing shadows, but they slowed to a walk.

Tap's clothes were soaked to the bone; he could feel the water standing in his boots.

This is gettin' bad, Andrews. What are you tryin' to prove? You're just too stubborn to admit these two drovers were right. Only a complete fool would go on like this. It's a dangerous thing when a man's stubbornness makes him act like a fool.

With his leather gloves wringing wet and his beaver felt hat sagging and beginning to seep, he circled Brownie and the other horses off the road to the right, just past the crossroad to Salt Lake, and drew up in a clump of scrub cedars.

"Well, boys, you win. We need a fire, and I figure if we can find some dry cedar, we'll be lucky. It's a solid bet there isn't any more wood for the next twenty miles."

Within half an hour a snapping, smoking fire lit up the stormy night as the three men, two still hand-tied, clustered around for warmth.

"I'm a little warmer, Deputy," Primo reported. "So you might as well let us go now."

Tap glanced across the fire with the rifle in his lap pointed their direction. The rain halted, but a cold wind blew with a frigid, biting, dangerous howl. The muddy ground began to freeze.

"You got to let us go."

"How's that?"

"Well, you got two choices. You can shoot us—"

"Don't give him no ideas!" Petey protested.

"But he ain't goin' to shoot us. There ain't no reason to waste all this flame on us if he was plannin' on pluggin' us. So he has to let us go 'cause we done saw him lead down Jerome while he was still in the sack. That's murder. He can't let us go back to Cheyenne and tell folks what he's done."

"Jerome was tryin' to escape," Tap suggested.

"Escape? You had him bagged like a raccoon in a flour sack!"

"Yeah, but who's goin' to believe you two?"

"We'll tell 'em, won't we, Petey?"

"Then I guess you're right, Primo. I'll just have to shoot you," Andrews agreed.

"I won't tell 'em," Petey chimed in. "No, sir, I won't say a thing! Primo said he'd tell 'em, but I didn't say that. Did you hear me say that?"

"Shut up, Petey!" Primo growled. "He ain't shootin' us."

Tap didn't hear the wagons creak.

Or the horses snort.

Or the riders mumble.

But he saw the bullet hit the fire.

The first shot came from the darkness of the road and hit the firewood. Sparks flew over Tap, Primo, and Petey. They rolled for the cover of the Wyoming night.

"Put your guns down; we're comin' in!" a voice shouted.

Tap kicked the fire apart and dove behind what he hoped was a tree stump. A flash of gunfire—and splinters exploded from the stump. Tap threw the wet rifle to his shoulder, and his fire-warmed hands gripped the icy trigger and squeezed. He re-cocked the '73 at the same time he heard someone let out a curse and a scream.

Are these more friends of Jerome? They could have shot me and not the fire if they wanted to. I don't even know who they are or what they want, and I'm clippin' 'em already.

"Andrews, hold your fire!" a voice screamed above the howling wind. "You hit Eden in the arm!"

"You shot first!" Tap hollered and then changed positions.

"Wait! We just want you to put down your gun so we can talk, that's all. We didn't plan on wingin' ya."

"Who's we?"

"Just some citizens of Cheyenne who figure that Hager ought to pay for what he did."

"So do I. That's why we have judges and courts!"

"That ain't what we were hired to do."

"Who hired you?"

"We want to come in and get Hager. Then we'll leave you and the others to go your way. We just want to take Hager back to Cheyenne for his just deserts."

Why on earth would they want to take him back to town to hang him?

"You're out of luck, boys. You don't get Hager."

"We'll have to take him from ya. I suppose that means a couple of you will get killed."

"Wait!" Petey yelled from the darkness. "Don't shoot no more, boys. Hager's already dead! You cain't hang him now!"

"That's right," Primo called. "We seen Andrews shoot him while he was still tied and in a sack."

"Is that right, Andrews?"

Tap kept his rifle pointed in the direction of the voice, but he could hear horses circling around behind them. He scrambled to a better position with a ten-foot cedar in the shadows behind him.

"Andrews? This is Strappler from DelGatto's. Don't shoot. I want to talk to you. Let me light a torch, and I'll come in."

DelGatto's must be empty tonight.

"Take it easy, boys," Petey called. "He's got us tied up. There's two of us in here that was just ridin' up to work on the Bar 79 in Johnson County."

The winds died down. Tap could now hear the restless movement of men and horses. A few stars flickered through broken clouds, and he was able to see the faint outline of wagons and riders.

"Deputy!" he heard Petey whisper. "Don't let them hang us. That ain't right. Don't let that mob get us."

"Andrews?"

Tap saw the faint flicker of a glowing torch.

"It's me—Strappler. . . . Where are you? I need to talk to you. I put my gun up. See, I'm not carrying a pistol."

The torch inched its way down the slope toward the cedars and the few embers of the earlier campfire still visible.

"Where are you, Deputy?"

A cold, wet steel barrel of a '73 Winchester pressed against the man's neck. "Right behind you, Strappler!"

"Come on, Deputy, put that down! I want to—"

"You all right, Strap?" a voice from the road shouted.

"It's time to ride, boys. You aren't takin' any prisoners of mine."

"We been ridin' in this storm for hours—all the way to Swan's and back. We want Hager now."

"He'll stand trial and then get his due. I'm hopin' more than anyone that they'll hang him."

"We ain't hopin' he'll hang; we intend to see that it happens. Pappy weren't the only one to die in that shootout at the Occidental. You jist ride off, Deputy. We'll take care of these here," Strappler insisted.

"No!" Petey screamed. "I told ya, we're jist drovers headin' north. Hager is already dead. Look on that black horse!"

Strappler strained to look behind him. "Is that true? Did you already kill Hager?"

"I said he would stand trial," Andrews insisted.

"He cain't stand trial if he's dead. He's dead, we tell you!" Primo screamed.

"Show us the body, and we'll light shuck," Strappler promised.

"Show 'em, Deputy!" Primo called.

Several men moved toward the horses. A number of them now carried torches. Their flushed faces reflected bizarre patterns in the flickering light.

"Look," Andrews yelled. "I'll let Strappler check out the sack. Then you mount up and ride out of here. Now the rest of you back up!" He waved the '73 Winchester at the crowd.

"Take a look, Strap," a voice boomed from the west.

Strappler carried the torch while Tap pressed the '73 to the back of his neck. They moved toward the horses.

"Keep a distance, boys. Strappler's in a tight spot here."

As they approached the horses, several of the mob crept closer.

"Untie it and shove it to the ground," Tap instructed as they approached the black horse with the white blaze on his nose.

"Okay, Strappler, open the sack and tell 'em what you find."

The night manager at DelGatto's dug hurriedly through the sack.

"This isn't anything but a bunch of bricks and blankets!"

"What do you mean?" Petey shouted. "We saw him—"

"Blankets? Bricks? Where's Hager?"

"Hager isn't here!" Tap called out. "He never has been."

"Ain't there? We saw Andrews smuggle Jerome out of town in that sack!" Petey protested.

"The freighter didn't have him at Swan's. We done checked there," one of the men reported.

"Merced said he wasn't in the jail."

Merced is connected with this gang?

"Where is he, Andrews?"

A deep voice shouted, "We want justice!"

"No, you don't want justice. You want vengeance. Vengeance belongs to the Lord, but He expects us to take care of justice."

Several men with guns in hand crowded closer to Andrews.

"Deputy, if you know what's good for you, you'll tell where he is!" came another threat.

Tap whirled toward the speaker, and while the others stood and stared, he jammed the barrel of his cocked '73 Winchester rifle into the man's chest. "Are you threatenin' me, mister?" he growled. "'Cause if my life is in danger, I'll just pull this trigger right now!"

"Wait!" the man sniveled. "I was—it was . . ."

"While you boys are playin' vigilante out here, Hager could be in Laramie City or Denver or Pine Bluffs or Ft. Collins or Rawlins. Now I'm loadin' up these prisoners and ridin' back to town. If I see even one of you in the shadows, I'm goin' to shoot! Do you understand?"

"These two were with Hager, weren't they? Maybe we ought to just haul them back to town and hang them!" a short man with a long beard taunted.

The barrel of Tap's rifle crashed against the man's head, and he dropped motionless to the ground.

"Petey and Primo weren't part of that ruckus at the Occidental. So anyone else plan on talkin' about hangin'?"

"You had no cause to . . ." The voice grew silent at Tap's glare.

He's probably right. Lord, there's got to be a better way of doin' this job than bashin' in skulls and shootin' all of 'em.

"Load this one up, and the rest of you get out of here."

They dragged the man back to their horses and wagons.

"We could have got the drop on him," someone murmured.

Tap thought he heard Strappler reply, "Providin' six of us want to die doin' it."

In the black of night, he heard horses whinny and wagons roll south toward Cheyenne.

An hour later Petey, Primo, and Tap could see the incandescent street lights of Cheyenne.

"Them new Edison lights is a pretty sight—even if it does mean jail," Petey remarked. "How do you figure Cheyenne's the first town in the whole dang country to get 'em?"

"Lots of rich folks in Cheyenne. They get what they want," Tap replied.

"Are they the ones tryin' to lynch Jerome?" Primo questioned.

"I don't figure it's the locals. For some reason this one bunch of bummers seems bent on turnin' the devil loose on Cheyenne. I don't aim to let that happen."

"You stood 'em down for us. We're much obliged to you for that, Deputy," Petey added.

"You know," Primo continued, "we've cowboyed with old Jerome on several roundups and drives, but we really ain't all that close."

"He's too wild to spend time with in town, if you know what I mean," Petey joined in.

"It's jist that those bummers stirred things up the other day. If they'd stayed down in their own territory, none of this would have ever happened, and the marshal would still be alive. It don't seem fair that they stir it up, and Jerome has to pay the whole invoice," Primo concluded.

"Yeah," Petey put in. "By this time we would've been pullin' out with the roundup wagons."

"You boys really have jobs at the Bar 79?"

"Yes, sir, we do."

"When's their wagon pullin' out?"

"They was hopin' to send an early crew out tomorrow—weather permittin'."

"Is TwoHoots the wagon-boss still?"

"Yep. He's the one who hired us."

"When we get to town, I'll stick you in jail. In the mornin' I'll contact TwoHoots and see if he'll bail you out. If he comes and pays your fine, I'll ask the judge to send you out on that Bar 79 wagon. But I don't want to catch you in Cheyenne for a year. Is that clear?"

"Deputy, if you can get us off to ride with that wagon, you'll never see us ever. Right, Petey?"

"That's a fact! But what about Jerome?"

"Jerome's goin' to pay for what he did. There's no escapin' that. I'll work to see he gets what he deserves, boys. That's fair, isn't it?"

"Yes, sir, I guess it is."

"You ain't tryin' to just bluff us into jail with this talk, are ya?" Primo asked.

"Boys, if I say I'm goin' to shoot you, you can bank on it. I'll shoot you. And if I tell you I'll turn you over to Bar 79, well, I'll turn you loose. And if you come lookin' for me instead of leavin' town, I can guarantee I'll gun you down on the spot. You catch my drift?"

"Yes, sir, we do."

Neither man said another word, even when Tap locked them in a jail cell about an hour before daylight. By the time he put up his horses at the I-X-L Livery and hiked to his house, the evening sky had turned grayish blue, and the wind blew cold from the north.

Baltimore Gomez met him at the front door. He was Tap's height but about thirty solid pounds heavier and always a week late with a shave. He fooled many about the speed of his gun and his resolve to pull the trigger.

"Ever'thing safe here?" Tap asked.

"Ain't heard a peep out of no one," Baltimore reported. "Even Hager's been sleepin'. How about you? You look like you're runnin' down faster than a dollar watch."

"Well, I do feel like I've been rode hard and put away wet. I brought in a couple of Hager's friends. They're over at the jail. But that lynch mob was mighty disappointed they couldn't find old Jerome."

"Did you have to throw lead?"

"Oh, I think I winged one and coldcocked another. It wasn't much of a fight."

"Tap, for most of us, that would be counted as a real shootout. 'Course, if they find out you got Jerome over here, you'll have quite a scrape."

"That's for sure. Baltimore, go home and get some sleep."

"I been sleepin' all night. But I would like to get me some breakfast and check on Angelita. I'll come back in a couple hours and see how you're doin'."

"Thanks, partner. . . . Remember, don't tell anyone Hager's over here—not Angelita and especially not Merced."

"Was Simp with the lynch mob?"

"Nope, but he and DelGatto seemed to be their main sources of information."

"You know him and Alex DelGatto moved to town about the same time last December. But Simp claims he didn't know DelGatto before."

"He spends a lot of time over there every night. It's the same crowd of loafers and bummers. The honest pilgrims have just about all moved on up to the Black Hills."

"What do you suppose that bunch is waitin' around fer?"

"I don't know, Baltimore. It's almost like they figured a lynchin' was about to happen."

Gomez hitched up his suspenders and jammed on a floppy brown hat. "It's all yours, partner." He tipped his hat, pulled on his coat, and left.

Tap watched Baltimore walk to the corner. He saw the curtain flutter in the upstairs window of the house across the street.

I wonder how long it will be before Mrs. Wallace tells someone what's goin' on over here?

He stepped to the back room and checked on Hager. Returning to the front room, he sat down on the floor near the woodstove and leaned against the sofa. Within minutes he was asleep.

The thing Pepper liked most about Cheyenne was that everyone saw her as Mrs. Andrews, the wife of a hard-working deputy marshal. To people around town she wasn't a dance-hall girl. Nor a former dance-hall girl.

True, she wasn't a part of Cheyenne's elite society. But she wasn't one of the girls across the tracks either. She wasn't a maid working in one of the big Victorian homes. She didn't take in laundry for the troops at Ft. Russell. Nor did she have to clean at the downtown hotels where they stacked four to six cowboys per room until the spring ranch work began.

She and Tap held a place on the lower end of Cheyenne's middle class. She was just the lady who lived in the little bungalow down the street and bought groceries on Fridays and Mondays, attended the Baptist church with her husband, and took rides in the country with him on Sunday afternoons.

Dozens of men passed her on the street each day, tipping their hats in respect, but not one of them made suggestive remarks. It was a refreshing, satisfying freedom she had never known before.

Pepper liked it.

She even accepted Tap's job as deputy.

That is, until Pappy Divide got shot in the back.

Sitting in the front parlor of Suite G at the Inter Ocean Hotel, she waited for Savannah to dress.

Lord, I don't know how she does it. She carries on with the sorrowful acceptance that this is her burden in life. But surely no one is called to be widowed three times, are they?

Gracious in sorrow.

Hopeful in despair.

Confident in confusion.

Maybe it IS a calling.

But, Lord, I'm sure it's not my calling!

"Pepper, tell me the truth. Does this jewelry look too flashy for a grieving widow? Be honest!" Savannah seemed to float across the room.

"Well, it's . . . it's beautiful, Savannah. I don't think it's in any way disrespectful, if that's what you mean."

"It was Pappy's favorite. He bought this necklace for me in St. Louis. My, that man had good taste in jewelry!"

"He was a real gentleman, wasn't he? Tap had worked for him only three days when he came home and said, 'Pepper, someday I'm goin' to be like Pappy.'"

"You know what Pappy said after the first time he met Mr. Andrews? 'He's a straight-shooter, Savannah.' You know, that's the highest compliment he ever gave any man." Standing in front of an etched-glass mirror, she held silver and black earrings alongside her face. "Then you think it would be all right to wear this jewelry to the undertaker's?"

"Savannah, there's not one person in this town—not even Mrs.

Swan, Mrs. Van Tassell, or Mrs. Carey—who would begrudge you to wear that jewelry if you want to."

"Thanks, honey. I value your opinion more than most of the others."

Pepper stood and brushed down her dark gray dress with her hand. "Oh, why is that?" She always felt so plain and boring around Savannah, yet she enjoyed being with her immensely.

Savannah slipped on her cape and held the door open for Pepper. "Well, let's just say there's a truth in your tone that comes from a life that has seen lies . . . and a joy in your eyes that comes from years of knowing sadness."

Pepper stared at Savannah in silence.

What does she know about me?

"Does it surprise you that I said that?"

"Well, I . . . eh . . ."

"It's true, isn't it? That's all right, honey. It's kind of a discernment thing that the Lord gives me. I just don't make mistakes when it comes to judging people. But don't worry—I have no curiosity to find out what you had to go through to reach this place. I enjoy you as a friend. That's all I ever need to know."

Pepper followed Savannah down the swooping staircase into the lobby and out onto the boardwalk.

"I guess I've never known anyone quite like you," Pepper finally responded. She thought she noticed a smile under the black veil that hung from Savannah's hat.

"Well, honey, others have told me that—some with a blessing and some with a curse."

Savannah and Pepper sat in the viewing room at the undertaker's and stared at Pappy Divide. He was stretched out in a polished oak coffin. Savannah's black gloved hands were folded in her lap. Her face seemed to show no emotion.

After several minutes Pepper brushed back a tear and sighed. She reached over and took Savannah's hand.

"Are you doing all right?"

The lady in black took a deep breath. "I was just telling Pappy we should have taken that trip to California last winter like I said."

"I guess you think about all those things you didn't do."

"And all the things we did! Pappy liked to travel. But somehow in every town we would end up at the sheriff's or marshal's office to visit old friends. He must have known every lawman and every lawbreaker west of the Mississippi."

"Did he know many down in Arizona and New Mexico?" Pepper tried to sound casual.

"Well, he knew Pat Garret, Stuart Brannon, at least four Earp brothers, and some of those . . . why?"

"Oh . . . nothing. Eh," Pepper mumbled, "Tap used to live in Arizona, and I thought they might have had some mutual friends."

"Well, perhaps they did. Pappy never mentioned it. You know, I certainly hope the council has enough sense to appoint Mr. Andrews acting marshal."

"The mayor appointed him temporary acting marshal."

"Well, that's good. I'm sure Pappy would have approved. Is your Tap planning on running for marshal?"

"He's talked about it a little. But I'm not sure what he decided."

"Well, you tell him I think he's a fine man, but I don't think he should run for the permanent position."

"Why's that?"

"For one thing, from what I hear, he's just too good a gunman. That will attract every derelict with a gun for a thousand miles. Besides, I've been married to the past three marshals in this town, and he's just not the right type."

"Oh?" Pepper strained to look past the veil at Savannah's eyes. "Just what is the right type?"

"Unmarried!" Savannah flashed a quick, temporary smile.

After supper at the crowded hotel dining room, Pepper and Savannah retired to the parlor of Suite G where they entertained a steady stream of visitors expressing sympathy. Everyone from Mrs. William Hale—the territorial governor's wife—to Mr. and Mrs. J. Slaughter—the superintendent of public instruction and his wife, to Chang Lee and his six sons, to Franklin Moran of the I-X-L, to Rev. and Mrs. Brewster.

Pepper's role was to open the door and usher the guests in, then sit in the green velvet arm chair near the window, and watch Savannah converse with style, faith, and grace.

Most discussions were the same. Everyone would mention Savannah's repeated misfortune and their great appreciation for all that Pappy did for the community. Only once did Pepper feel awkward, and that was when Raelynn Royale, owner of the Royale Palace stopped by. Pepper remembered Raelynn as Clara Johnston, a girl she had once worked with in Boise City. Fortunately, peering out through heavy make-up and a mountainous black, curly wig, Raelynn didn't recognize Pepper.

One thing everyone agreed upon was that Jerome Hager should receive swift, irrevocable justice. It was well after 10:00 P.M. before the last guest departed and the ladies prepared for bed.

"Pepper, honey, you've got to give Mr. Andrews a big hug of thanks for allowing you to stay with me awhile. Nights are going to be the most difficult part, you know. Over and over and over I will be waking up thinking that I hear Pappy coming in. I'll hear him call my name. I'll smell his clothes or his lotion . . . and I'll convince myself he's still here. I guess having gone through it before helps me know that somehow I will survive. The Lord is always sufficient in that way. But it also means I know exactly how painful the process will be."

"Savannah, you're so strong. I can't believe how well you handled all the callers."

"Strong? Honey, I'm just going through the motions by habit. I've done it all before. Right now I think I'd like to have a cup of tea . . . a real good cry . . . and then stare at a dark ceiling for a few hours."

Savannah's jet-black hair was always meticulously in place tucked into her combs. The posture was perfect. Her smile was a permanent Cheyenne fixture. To Pepper her bearing was almost regal.

In another era she'd be a duchess or a queen . . . or something.

Only her eyes reflected a crushing sadness. "What can I do to help?" Pepper asked.

"How about you fetching us both a cup of tea."

Pepper slept sporadically in Savannah Divide's folding bed. Her thoughts bounced from Pappy to Tap, and she prayed repeatedly for his safety.

She arose early and slipped on a fluffy burgundy robe that Savannah had laid out for her. Standing at the window of the second-floor suite, she stared out at the Cheyenne sunrise.

Lord, there's got to be other things that Tap can do. I don't think I can . . . I don't want him to . . . I mean, some drunk will shoot him in the back someday and . . . He could always get a job as . . . or maybe he could . . . He's a hard worker. He's got lots of experience at . . .

Lord, You've just got to give him a ranch.

Six blocks away Tap was glad his eyes flipped open shortly before 8:00 A.M., but he didn't know why they did. With little more than two hours of sleep, his bones were cold and stiff, and his mind was groggy.

It's almost like someone nudged me awake. Primo and Petey! I promised to get them before a judge this morning!

He stirred the fire and boiled some coffee. Jerome Hager sprawled across the brass bed snoring loudly.

"This is crazy," Tap muttered. "He kills Pappy, and he gets a good night's sleep, and me—I freeze to death in that storm and sleep a couple of hours on the floor." He was splashing water on his face when someone knocked at the door.

With revolver in hand, Tap pushed back the curtains. Baltimore surveyed the nearly empty street from the front step. Tap let the deputy in.

"What are you doin' back already?" he quizzed.

"I got full! Besides 16th Street is swarmin' with that lynch mob that's been drinkin' ever since you run 'em back to town. I figured you'd want to know."

"I'd like to know who rented the horses and rigs for them and who's buyin' the booze. Other than Strappler, they didn't look like they had six guns or six dollars between the whole pack of them. What do you have in the basket?"

"Lunch. And a little breakfast for Hager. Told Angelita I'd be gone 'til supper. Where do you need me most?"

"Right here. I've got to find Judge Blair and see what can be done about Hager and the others."

"Sooner or later someone will figure out where you're hidin' Hager, don't you reckon? Did you know that old lady across the street watches this place like a cow eyein' her young at a brandin'?"

"Yep."

Tap ate a couple of biscuits and hiked over to the jail. Carbine Williams was drinking coffee from a blue tin cup on the front steps as he approached. His crisp, long-sleeved, off-white cotton shirt contrasted with the grimy jeans.

"Things have been poppin' since you brought them two in," Carbine reported.

"You have early mornin' visitors?"

"Simp Merced came in cussin' and snortin'. Threatened to shoot them two if they didn't tell him where Hager was."

"What happened?"

"Just noise. He didn't shoot 'em. They claimed you was the only one who knew where Hager was."

"Who else came by?"

"The mayor said to tell you he had to go to Denver."

"I thought they were having a council meeting tonight."

"He said he was going to postpone it. Some sort of family emergency. Ain't his daughter in the hospital down there? I heard tell that sanatorium is one of the best in the country."

Tap brushed biscuit crumbs from his bushy, dark brown mustache. "You didn't happen to see Judge Blair, did you?"

"Nope."

"Is Simp makin' rounds?"

"Don't know, but he acted like there was demons chasin' him. You know how he can git."

"I never thought of it that way," Tap mused. "But you might be right." Andrews walked out of the marshal's office and across the limestone steps to the courthouse.

Is that what does it, Lord? Don't reckon I've ever pondered it too much, but men like Jordan Beckett, Billy Bonney, Carter Dillard—they get driven beyond reasonable actions. Maybe demons have somethin' to do with it. . . . 'Course, Pepper says I always make things bigger than they are. But sometimes it surely feels prickly to my spirit.

Judge James Arthur Blair was at his bench discussing a case with two bummers when Tap slipped into the back of the courtroom. He flopped into an oak chair and waited.

The taller of the two ill-dressed and unshaven men was speaking. "You see, Judge, when me and Nickles left Omaha, we signed this agreement that we were going to share expenses and equally divide any and all gold, silver, and other riches we might discover. See . . . I got his signature right here."

"I didn't agree to share expenses with an idiot!" Nickles complained. He held a derby in his hand that looked like a bite had been taken out of it.

"Eh . . . just how did you say you two are related?"

"He married my wife's baby sister—poor thing!"

The sister-in-law or this guy?

"Your Honor, he agreed to share expenses. This here certificate gives us twenty-two feet of the Crystal Cave Mine. I bought it for $10, and now he won't fork over his five dollars."

The judge looked at the large certificate with fancy print.

"Where did you buy this?" he asked.

"From a little, dark-haired girl down at the U. P. Station. She said her granddaddy was dying, and they needed the money to take him to Virginia."

The one called Nickles waved his finger at the certificate. "It's worthless, ain't it, Judge?"

"Yes, it's worthless." Then Judge Blair looked out across an otherwise empty courtroom. "Deputy Andrews!"

Tap stood and took off his hat. "Yes, sir?"

"Have you talked to Angelita about this yet?"

"Yes, sir. I did. She reassured me yesterday that she would no longer sell mining certificates at the station."

"Thank you . . ."

"I told you it wasn't worth a penny. I ain't payin' jist because you got suckered!"

"You agreed. I got it in writin'!"

"Boys," the judge interrupted, "let me teach you a couple of things. First, half of the stock certificates and mining claims you're going to find in this town are legitimate claims to worthless property. You can buy twenty feet of a mine that will never be dug because there is no ore there. Second, the other half are like this one —just pulp that was printed down on 12th Street. You should have known better. Look right there in big letters— 'Deadwood, Wyoming Territory.' Every schoolboy in the country knows that Deadwood is in Dakota. Obviously this is a phony."

"Well, I'll be. But . . . but I need the money, Judge. I'm down to my last two bits. I need that five dollars."

"I ain't got five extree dollars," Nickles fumed. "If I had that kind of money, I'd go to Denver, and you know it. That's where the real fortunes are made."

The judge banged down his gavel. "Case dismissed. Boys, let me give you some advice. Don't go to Deadwood. You'll starve to death up there. You're six years too late. The ranch crews will be pulling out this week. You two ever worked cattle?"

"Only a dairy farm back in Omaha," Nickles admitted.

"Well, you could sign on as a nighthawk or hoodlum and at least get something to eat, and come summer you'd have enough money for a train ride home."

"I should never have listened to you. My wife was right about you!" Nickles screamed.

"I want you out of my courthouse, or I'll ask the deputy to incarcerate you immediately!" the judge threatened.

"Incarcerate?"

"Tossed in the hoosegow, you idiot!" The other shoved his way out of the courtroom.

The judge shook his head. "Don't ever become a judge, Andrews."

"Not me, sir."

"Well, Mr. Acting Marshal, are you here about Hager?"

"Temporary acting marshal. Yes, sir, I'm here about Hager. And about a couple boys who broke some windows in the jail to get him out."

"Let's start with the easy ones. What about those two men?"

"This is just my suggestion," Tap explained, "but I'd like to have you fine them expenses and sentence them to six months in jail, which will be suspended providin' they pull out with the Bar 79 today and do not set foot in Cheyenne for a year."

The judge leaned back in his brown leather chair.

"What's your reason for that?"

"There's a pack of bummers that is gettin' lynchy. They are mostly out for revenge against the drovers. But being that Pappy was killed in the shootout, there's lots of folks around town that will support them. I think they might even try hangin' Hager's friends if they can't get to Hager. I'd just like to get these boys out of town so I won't have to protect them. They have jobs on the Bar 79, and TwoHoots will pay their fine."

"Sounds good to me. Bring them before me at . . ." Judge Blair checked his gold-chained pocket watch. "At ten o'clock. You sure you're not looking to be a judge?"

"Yes, sir. I'm sure I'm not."

"Hager's a problem, all right. I haven't seen folks in this town so stirred up since those four girls at the Paris Club got knifed to death."

"I've got him in a secured place now, but I'm not sure how long I can keep him there. The jail isn't safe."

"Is he still in the city?" the judge questioned.

Tap glanced around. Two people walked into the back of the courtroom.

"Yes, sir," he said quietly under his breath.

"You got witnesses to the crime?"

"Yep. Rolly Hayburn saw Hager shoot Pappy in the back when that gunfight was nearly over."

"Was Rolly sober?"

"He was after the shootin'."

"Is Hager pleading guilty?"

"He claims he was drunk and doesn't remember anything."

"A man's totally responsible for all his actions, drunk or not. If he demands a jury trial, he'll get a jury trial. Bring him here at 11:00 A.M., and I'll set a trial date. In the meantime, I believe I'll ask the commanding officer at Ft. Russell if he can escort Hager to their stockade to await the trial."

"I reckon Governor Hale won't be too pleased you had to call in federal troops."

"The governor's out of the territory. I believe I can summon the troops for official court business. I'm talking about public safety. It's not a time to worry about politics. Andrews, I don't want to know where you're keeping him. Just have him here in my court-room at 11:00."

"Yes, sir, I will."

"You've kept him alive longer than I figured," the judge added. "I didn't reckon he'd make it through the night."

4

Tap fastened the top buttons of his worn canvas coat and scrambled down the courthouse steps. He hurried south on Ferguson Street. His boot heels banged decisively on the boardwalk. Tipping his hat to Mrs. Matthews and her baby, he waited for the Gilroy and Hannigan wagons and riders to pass before crossing 17th.

Well, at least some of the cowhands are leavin' Cheyenne.

Half a dozen men lounged around the entrance to the Inter Ocean Hotel. Their fogged-breath conversations ceased as Andrews drew near. He didn't bother acknowledging their stares but pushed his way into the warm, stuffy lobby. He could feel most folks inside studying his movements as he ascended the stairs.

I suppose ever'one in town knows I'm hidin' Jerome somewhere. I've got to get him out of the house today. There's just too many folks in town with nothin' to do except stir up a ruckus.

The wide door of Suite G swung open revealing what he considered to be the prettiest blonde-haired woman in the Territory.

"Mornin', babe." He winked.

Pepper broke into a wide grin. "Mornin', Deputy." She slipped her arms around his waist and tugged him into the room, closing the door behind them.

"How's Savannah doin'?" he asked.

"She's a rock. There's no woman in Wyoming like Savannah Divide."

"That's what Pappy always said."

Pepper kissed his chapped lips and stepped back. "You look tired, honey."

"I had a long night."

"Everything go all right?"

"I think so. Judge Blair is goin' to help me figure out something with Hager. I'm goin' to move him out of the house this afternoon so you can go back home."

"Do you think I could stay with Savannah one more night? She seems to appreciate it immensely."

"Sure. Only you'll have one lonesome husband."

There was a soft, teasing lilt in her voice. "Good!" She took him by the arm and walked him over to the window. "Listen, there's a Calico Hop out at Ft. Russell tomorrow night. The marshal and his wife are always invited, so Savannah thinks you and I ought to go. What do you think?"

"There's no way to think about a dance with all of this goin' on."

"I told her you wouldn't be interested."

"I didn't say I wasn't interested. If Pappy hadn't been shot and me guardin' the—"

"If Pappy hadn't been shot, we wouldn't be invited," Pepper interrupted. "The point is, you're acting marshal, and it might be a good time to get to know the officers out at the fort."

Tap stood with his arms folded in front of him and stared through the thin lace modesty curtain that was framed in deep blue velvet. He watched the rigs roll past on the street below. "I do need to talk to them about guardin' Hager."

"Savannah said I could wear the new calico dress she had made for the dance."

"Are you sure it's not some deceivin' scheme to get me to wear a ruffled shirt?" Tap feigned a scowl.

"You can wear anything you want to," she offered.

"Really?"

"Well, you know . . . within reason."

"Whose reason?"

"Mine, of course!" Pepper's laugh sent a tingle right down Tap's spine.

"If things settle down, and if we get Hager situated, I guess we could attend the ball for a while. Are you sure we'd be invited?"

"I've got the invitation right here." She handed him the gold-embossed card.

Tap glanced at the print. "Looks like they need reservations. You'd better send word to the Fort that we'll be comin'."

Pepper tossed her arms around him and pressed her lips against his. "I already did," she mumbled.

It was a good five minutes before she pulled away from him.

Tap pushed his way through the tall, windowless doors of the Drovers' Cafe. About seventy-five men crowded around twelve tables, each trying to snag a plate of breakfast. The room smelled of bacon, tobacco, and sweat. Large pictures of racehorses were scattered among paintings of reclining ladies.

TwoHoots sat with his back to the wall and a fork in each hand. The jingle of Andrews's spurs could barely be heard above the scraping of tin plates and the slurping of black coffee.

"You goin' to let my boys pull out with the wagon?" the crew boss of the Bar 79 mumbled through a mouthful of biscuits and pork sausage gravy.

"You pay court expenses and jail costs, and Petey and Primo can go with you today. Be at Judge Blair's chambers at 10:00."

"You goin' to let me talk to Jerome? You know, talk around town is maybe one of them loafers or bummers shot the marshal and jist blamed it on Hager 'cause he was too drunk to know better. They been tryin' to pick a fight for weeks, and you know it."

The voices around the room grew hushed. Tap could see a few hands slip down and rest on their holstered revolvers. The fire popped and crackled in the woodstove. It was as if everyone in the room stopped eating at exactly the same moment.

"There's a few witnesses who say different. Jerome's safe and comfortable. You can't talk to him yet, TwoHoots, but you can sure enough hire him a lawyer if you want to."

"I heard those bummers came into the Occidental lookin' for a fight."

"That might be, but Pappy didn't. It seems like some of the boys in this room got the idea that back-shootin' a marshal ain't a serious crime."

"How about back-shootin' a deputy?" A deep voice filtered across the room.

Tap whipped around. Most of the crowd were still seated at tables, although several stood at the back wall with their coattails tucked behind their revolvers.

"I hope one of you five at this front table said that!" he growled.

"Don't look at us, Deputy. We're jist sittin' here eatin' our biscuits and eggs."

"Well, that's too bad because if even one shot is fired in this room, you five will be the first I shoot. Don't figure I could miss from this range. It would be a shame for you to take lead for some loudmouthed jerk in the back row that doesn't have the guts to face me one to one, wouldn't it?"

"Who you callin' a loudmouthed jerk?" A big man with a full beard stood up at the back of the room, his hand on his revolver. His belly hung over an empty bullet belt.

"It looks like you're the one, partner. Now sit down and put your hands above the table before you go do something foolish and prove my words about you!"

The man sat right down.

Tap glanced around at the rest in the room. "Let's get somethin' straight, boys. I don't favor those bummers down at the track. I don't work for the rich folks in those three-story houses, and I don't automatically side with driftin' cowhands who spend only three weeks a year in town. If someone commits a crime, they ought to be fairly punished . . . that's all. Don't matter who they are.

"But you might as well know, I won't hesitate to draw this gun and shoot any one of you in this room if needs be to uphold the law. I don't scare. I don't back down. And there is nothin' in the world that riles me more than someone threatenin' me. I haven't spent my whole life wearin' a badge. You all understand what I'm sayin'?"

"Yes, sir," a man in the front row said nodding. "Just one thing, Deputy—we could use a man like you up in Johnson County. You be interested in rollin' out with us?"

The tension in the room melted. Most of the drovers roared with laughter.

Andrews cracked a smile and walked to the door. "If you got a coosie that makes good bear sign, I might just look you up."

Simp Merced met Andrews on the boardwalk in front of the Drovers' Cafe. "What were you doin' in there?" he demanded.

Tap walked on by. "Talkin' to TwoHoots."

"Where's Hager? You got to tell me where you're keepin' him! It ain't right that I'm a deputy and don't even know what's goin' on!"

"Count it a blessin'. That way no one will threaten you at the Drovers' Cafe or ambush you on the trail."

"Andrews . . . you listen to me!" Merced grabbed Tap's arm.

One fiery glare caused Merced to drop his grip and step back. "I'm goin' to take this up with the city council. This is no way to run the marshal's office!"

"Yeah, you talk to 'em, Simp. You talk to 'em."

Andrews sat at the counter of S. S. Ramsey's restaurant on 16th Street drinking a cup of coffee and scraping up the last of his eggs.

A young voice called out from the door, "Hey, mister, you want to buy thirty prime feet of the Lost Gulch Mine?"

He spun around. Angelita stood giggling at the door.

"I thought I told—"

"Mr. Andrews," she lectured, "must you take everything so seriously? You really should relax and enjoy life more. You are much more handsome when you smile. That continual frown is quite unbecoming."

Tap broke into a wide grin and shook his head. "Judge Blair is just about ready to run you out of town, young lady."

"It's a sad world when children are victimized by our own legal system," she pouted.

"Children? You haven't acted like a child in ten years!"

"Well, then, a true gentleman wouldn't leave a beautiful, young woman standing at the door of a restaurant. He'd invite her in and offer to buy her a cup of coffee and a sweet roll."

"A glass of milk and a sweet roll," he corrected her.

"Whatever!" Angelita scampered into the cafe and leaped up on the stool beside him. "I want one of those big cinnamon ones with the sticky stuff and nuts on top!"

Andrews nodded approval to the waitress and laid a couple of coins on the counter. "You'll have to get along without my company. I have some marshalin' to do," he informed her.

"I don't know how I'll ever survive without you at my side, my dearest!" She held her hands under her head and faked a swoon.

He put his hand on her head and tousled her hair. "Be good."

"It's boring." She frowned. "Where's my daddy? I need to talk to him."

Tap stood to leave. "He's workin' and can't be bothered right now."

"I have to see him!" she insisted. "It's extremely important."

"I'll send him home about two."

"That will be too late. Do you have a dollar I may borrow?"

"What for?"

"I need to pick up some printing, and I must have the money by noon."

"Printing? What kind of printing?"

"I'm certainly not going to give away valuable business secrets in a public establishment like this!" she huffed. "Do I get the dollar or not?"

"No."

"Then perhaps I should go to your house and sit on the steps and cry until some kind person shows mercy on me."

Tap stared at Angelita's coal-black dancing eyes. "I know where Hager is," she mouthed without uttering a sound.

Lord, have mercy on all the little boys.

He tossed a dollar coin on the counter and walked out the front door.

It took less than ten minutes for Judge Blair to sentence, fine, suspend sentence, and release both Primo and Petey into TwoHoots's custody. Tap rode behind the Bar 79 crew all the way to the north edge of town and only turned back when they dropped over the dark, cloudy horizon.

Back at the jail Carbine Williams slouched on the front steps rolling a quirley.

"Who's spyin' out the jail, Carbine?"

"There's a couple drovers that have been standin' a long time in the cold on 19th Street. . . . And two loafers are sittin' on the steps of the Catholic church over there. I suppose both will send runners if they see Hager around the courthouse. How are you goin' to get him here?"

"I'm not sure, but go ahead and turn the drunks out. Empty the jail. Then scoot up to the roof of the courthouse with that '73 and a box of shells. Keep out of sight until the time comes."

"Which side am I supposed to shoot at?"

"Neither, I hope. What we want to do is get Hager into the courtroom. Whoever tries to prevent that will have to be dealt with. The judge is tryin' to bring in some soldier boys from the Fort to help out, so we shouldn't have any trouble once they arrive."

Tap rode down to the south side of the tracks where he found Simp Merced talking to some men in front of Alex DelGatto's saloon and dance hall.

"Simp, I need to talk to you," Tap called.

"What about?"

"Marshal business."

Simp Merced meandered over to where Andrews sat on Brownie. The other men stopped their talking and watched Tap.

"Yeah . . . what is it?"

"I need you to go over to the Union Pacific Station and keep an eye on the waitin' room—especially anyone totin' a gun."

"You fixin' to move Hager out by train?"

Tap looked around at the others standing back on the sidewalk. "I didn't say that!"

"But—"

"I said nothin' about Hager," Tap protested under his breath. "All you know is that you need to make the lobby safe."

"Oh . . . sure. I see." Simp nodded. "Well, it's about time you pulled me in on this. How long until you bring Hager . . . I mean, how much time do I have?"

"Thirty minutes. Can you do it?"

"You can count on me."

That's what I'm hopin', Simp. That's what I'm hopin'.

He rode through two back alleys and tied Brownie up to a once-white picket fence that ran along only one side of the back-yard of his house on 17th Street. He slipped around to the front door and knocked. Baltimore, with gun in hand, unhooked the latch and swung open the squeaking door.

"Lots of movement on the street—folks ridin' and walkin' by and gawkin'," he reported.

"Bummers or drovers?"

"Both."

"Any camped out on the street?"

Baltimore peeked out Pepper's lace curtains. "There's still someone in the attic of that house across the street. They've been watchin' yer house all mornin'."

"That's Mrs. Wallace. She stares at us every day."

"Nice neighbor. I don't know her. What's she look like?"

"Can't say." Tap shrugged. "She hasn't come out her front door in three months—as far as we can tell."

"And I thought things were strange on my side of town!" Baltimore grinned. "Now what's the plan?"

"Go over to the courthouse and take that double-barreled

12-gauge and stand right inside the front door by that granite column. Don't give anyone a chance to take a potshot at you. Carbine will be on the roof."

"What about Merced?"

"I sent him down to the train depot."

"What for?"

"To keep him out of the way."

"Did he fall for it?"

"I surely hope so."

"How long before you'll be bringin' Hager?"

"Tell the judge it will be about twenty, twenty-five minutes."

Baltimore looked up and down the sidewalk and then stepped out on the uncovered porch. Sticking his head back through the doorway, he asked, "How you goin' to do it, Tap? How you goin' to get Hager to the courthouse? You won't be able to get a buggy or wagon rollin' without everyone in town knowing about it. After that deal with the laundry wagon, every vehicle in town is suspect, and it's for dead certain they're watchin' the liveries."

"Maybe I'll just walk him down the middle of the street."

"That ought to save the city court costs. No, really . . . what are you goin' to do?"

"Whatever attracts as little attention as possible."

The carriage stopped abruptly on the narrow lane that ran down the middle of the graveyard. Two men in canvas bibbed coveralls crawled out of the hole they'd been digging. Hats in hand, they approached the rig.

"Mornin', Miz Savannah. We shore don't have no pleasure diggin' this one. Pappy always treated us square."

"Thank you, Clete. I just wanted to come by and see if the ground was too frozen or anything."

"No, ma'am. We made it through the frozen part without much trouble. We did get the right plot, didn't we? I mean, there's a whole string of 'em here that belongs to you."

"That's the one I had in mind. I don't suppose the stonemason will have anything ready by this afternoon?"

"He put aside his orders and promised to deliver it by two. It's just like these others, ain't it?"

"Yes. Only the names and dates change. You buried my Drake and my Quintin, didn't you, Clete?"

"Yes, ma'am. I surely hope I don't have to bury any more of your men."

"Thank you, Clete. That's certainly my hope also." Savannah glanced back at Pepper, who held the reins of the rented carriage. "Do you men know Mrs. Andrews?"

"Deputy Andrews's wife? Pleased to meet ya, ma'am."

"And I, you."

The shorter of the two surveyed Pepper. "I don't envy that husband of yours. Sort of like being trapped on the edge of a canyon cliff by a grizzly bear, I suppose."

"Mr. Andrews is one man in this town that can handle the situation," Savannah interjected.

"Yes, ma'am, I reckon he is. I surely pray I won't be needin' to dig a hole for him."

Savannah looked the man in the eyes. "That reminds me, Clete, your Myrtle says such wonderful prayers for you at church each Sunday. Just when are you going to get serious with God?"

Pepper noticed the startled look in Clete's eyes. *No one ever accused Savannah of being too subtle.*

"Well . . . ma'am . . . I, eh—you surely put me on the spot," he stammered.

"I intended to, Clete. I'm much too fond of you and Myrtle to let something so crucial slide by."

"I think . . . well, we ought to get back to work. I reckon I'll give it some thought."

"Good. We'll see you this afternoon." Savannah nodded at Pepper, who slapped the reins and drove the one-horse black buggy on down the lane.

Pepper held the reins in her gloved right hand and tried to brush her blonde hair back toward her hat. Her cheeks were cool, and she knew they had blushed red. "I think Clete was a little taken back by your boldness."

"Yes . . . well, he should be! You would think a man who

spends his time digging graves would be more concerned with his own eternal destiny."

"Savannah, have you always been so bold with your faith? I think I told you this is all pretty new to me."

"Bold? I'm a wallflower compared to my mother."

Her mother? Oh, dear!

"Pepper, darling, I figure you can either find yourself pushed along through life, or you can grab it by the reins and drive that sucker yourself. Lord willing, of course. And I aim to make the most of every day, every relationship, and every opportunity to share my faith. How about you? Are you just riding along in life, or are you driving?"

Pepper squirmed about on the black leather seat of the buggy. She didn't look at Savannah. "I guess I've spent most of my life being pushed and shoved. But lately . . . well, Tap and I have enjoyed learning to let the Lord lead us—if that's what you mean."

"Close enough."

Both women rode without speaking all the way back to the Bon Ton Livery on 18th and Eddy.

Lord, I always feel so inferior around Savannah. She knows how to talk to everyone in this town, no matter which side of the tracks they live on. She's not concerned what others say about her or what they think. Someday . . . someday, Lord, maybe I could be that way too. I mean, without losing a husband.

Pepper was surprised to see that no one was loitering in their customary positions around the livery. She did notice several men scurry toward 17th Street in the general direction of the U. P. Station.

"Is someone famous coming in on the train?" she asked the livery boy who took the reins and helped her and Savannah down.

"Leavin' town, I reckon. Word is that they'll try to send Jerome Hager out on the train. Some boys don't figure he'll ever get on board. The rest are jist goin' down to watch. Think I'll mosey down there myself. They say that deputy is gettin' himself in a real fix, ma'am. So I guess we'll see if he really has the sand for the job."

"That deputy happens to be Mrs. Andrews's husband." Savannah scowled. "And I can assure you he has enough sand to stand against the likes of the bummers and drovers in this town."

"Yes, ma'am . . . Miss Savannah." Then he turned to Pepper. "No offense, ma'am."

Pepper nodded but didn't say anything. She and Savannah walked arm in arm back toward the Inter Ocean Hotel.

"What do you suppose Mr. Andrews is up to, taking Hager to the train depot?" Savannah finally asked. "It sounds rather risky."

"Oh, I don't think Tap would take unnecessary risks . . . normally." *He always takes risks! Why can't he be more cautious like . . . well, like . . . like Pappy?*

Lord, keep him safe. Keep him safe right this minute. Please!

Pepper followed Savannah into Suite G at the Inter Ocean, then scooted straight to the window, and stared across town toward the Union Pacific Station.

"This ain't no way for a man to shave," Jerome Hager complained. "A man can't use a razor with both hands tied together and a cocked .44 pressin' into the back of his head."

"I want you to look your best for Judge Blair," Tap insisted.

"I don't see no reason to go advertising where my neck is," Hager groused. "Well, that's about as purdy as I get. When is the ambulance coming by?"

"You don't get a ride to the courthouse. We're walkin'."

"You're crazy, Andrews!" Hager shouted. "I ain't walkin' them streets."

"Now it's only about nine blocks. Even a deadbeat drover can walk that far."

"There's people out there that want to kill me! You said so yerself. That's why I've been hidin' in this here tiny shack of yours."

"There's people out there that want to kill me too," Tap reminded him.

"That's right! Old Petey and Primo will be waitin' to lead you down."

"I ran them out of town this mornin'. Surely you don't have any other friends in this town."

"Us drovers stick together. We're tired of them sneakthief and footpad bummers robbin' and knivin' and shootin' us and then gettin' away with it. It wouldn't surprise me if a whole passel of 'em will try and spring me."

"Then why are you worried about walkin' to the courthouse. Seems to me you have nothin' to worry about. Besides, I figure any friends you have left will be hangin' around the U. P. Station."

"How do you reckon?"

"Just a premonition. It'll be good for you to get out into some Cheyenne spring air."

"Yer goin' to untie my feet, ain't ya?"

"Yep. Just as soon as I lock these hand irons on both of us." He kept the pistol jammed into Hager's ribs as he fastened the hand irons.

"This don't make sense! We ain't really goin' to walk to the courthouse, are we?"

"Come on. This should be a memorable experience. Only I don't suppose you'll have time to write your memoirs. Go down the alley to Evans, then north to 19th, and west to the court-house."

"I can holler out, and they'll shoot you down," Hager threatened.

"Well, Jerome . . . I've looked around town the past couple of days, and I figure the odds are that if you shout, you'll take the first bullet. You willin' to call a shout and find out which one of us is right?"

"This is the stupidest thing I've ever done," Hager mumbled.

"Nope. The stupidest thing you ever did was shoot Pappy Divide in the back."

"I meant, this is the stupidest thing I ever done sober. I need a drink, Deputy. You got some liquor around the house?"

"Nope."

"Come on, Andrews. I might be dead in ten minutes. Surely you got a bottle stashed somewhere."

"No chance, Hager. Let's get this parade started."

"You ain't a deacon, are ya?"

"Not hardly. But I'll take that as a compliment."

Hager turned even more sullen as he stepped through the front door prodded by the barrel of Andrews's Colt .44. Tap surveyed the street back and forth as they walked east. When they turned north on Evans, a drover on a buckskin mare spun her around and galloped toward the tracks.

"He spotted us, Andrews. They'll be comin' after you now!"

"Or comin' after you. Keep walkin', Jerome."

"Look up there on the corner! Who's up there? Someone's waitin' for us."

"I reckon he is." Andrews walked straight up to the man.

"Tap, you need some help?" Rolly asked.

"How about you gettin' Brownie from behind my house and ride him up to the courthouse. I might need a pony to go out to Ft. Russell."

Rolly Hayburn scurried south, and Tap continued to march his prisoner north. Folks were now coming out on their front porches to watch the two men pass. A few could be seen scurrying downtown.

When they turned east on 19th, several riders scattered across Ransom Street. Andrews and Hager both stopped in their tracks when they saw Angelita running at them.

"What are you doin' here?" Andrews barked. "Go on. Get on home!"

"I'm going with you." Angelita turned to walk ahead of them.

"Listen to me—I'm tellin' you to go home. This is not a game to play!" Tap huffed. "Now I appreciate you wantin' to help me, but I—"

"Help you? Don't flatter yourself, Mr. Andrews. I bet Mr. Loo five dollars you could get Hager to the courthouse without either of you gettin' shot. There's a lot of bets being made."

"Where did you get five dollars?" Andrews demanded.

"I don't have it yet. That's why you've got to make it."

Her nose slightly in the air, her blue gingham dress dragging in the dirt, and her arms folded in front of her, ten-year-old Angelita led the two men down the middle of 19th Street.

Thirty or forty people now waited for them at the Ransom intersection. Most were cowboys on horseback, and many toted guns.

"Angelita, do you really want to help me get him there?"

"I want to win that bet," she replied.

"Well, here's what you do. Go on up and slip behind that crowd. If I give you a signal, run up to the courthouse and get your daddy and Carbine Williams to come down and bail me out."

"Really?"

"Yep. But don't go after them unless I signal you to."

"What kind of signal?"

"Just watch my eyes."

"I knew it." She grinned.

"Knew what?"

"I knew you couldn't get along without me! Can I skip?"

"Huh?"

"Everyone says I have a very cute skip!"

Angelita skipped toward the armed men on horseback. They spread apart to give her room. Most of the men smiled as they watched her.

Lord, keep her safe until she's old enough to know what she's got.

Then the men on horseback closed ranks. Two freight wagons full of roundhouse loafers and bummers rolled into the south side of the intersection. One was driven by cigar-chomping Alex DelGatto himself. Most carried axe handles or two-by-fours. A few sported old Henrys or cap-and-ball revolvers. The men on horseback swung to the north side of the intersection and faced off the men in the wagon. Andrews and Hager approached the middle of the intersection.

"Keep goin', Jerome," Tap muttered.

"This is insane! We're both dead. You know it, Deputy. There ain't no way to come out alive."

"Isn't this excitin', Hager? It surely beats being chained up in that bungalow of mine."

"Andrews, I don't know if you're the bravest man or the dumbest man I ever met!"

Lord, I've been wonderin' the same thing myself.

"Just stop right there, Deputy!" a man on horseback shouted. "There ain't no reason to go any further with this charade. Just unhitch Jerome, and we'll let you walk on out of here."

"I told ya I had friends!" Hager shouted.

"Give us some room, Andrews," one of the bummers shouted. "And we'll take care of Hager right now. No reason to kink a good rope when two hundred grains of lead will do the job."

"Listen up," Tap shouted, as he shoved Hager on down the street. "I can't turn Jerome loose. The key's at the jailhouse. Now we're walkin' down to the courthouse. This isn't a lawless gold camp. This is Cheyenne. We've got laws to follow. And I aim to see that we follow 'em."

"You ain't the only law in this town!"

Simp Merced burst out of the crowd near the wagons and stomped toward them.

"You lied to me, Andrews. You said you were takin' Hager to the depot."

"I didn't say a word about Hager, and you know it."

"You know what I mean." Merced pulled his gun out of the holster and kept coming right at Andrews.

Tap fought the urge to shoot Merced on the spot.

"This ain't good. This ain't no good at all!" Hager moaned.

"Keep walkin'. Absolutely don't stop for anything!" Andrews commanded under his breath. They brushed past Simp Merced.

"Andrews! I'll shoot you in the back if you don't stop!" he screamed.

For some reason, Tap thought about Pepper. He thought about how good it felt when they were walking down the boardwalk on 16th Street with their fingers laced in one another's. He thought about that sweet kiss of hers every morning when she came out to the kitchen and found him reading. He thought about how she clutched his arm tight whenever a pretty woman came within ten feet of him. He thought about their honeymoon on the ranch when the snowstorm trapped thirty people in the front room. He thought about the time he discovered her in the governor's office holding on to Carter Dillard. He thought about how sick to his stomach he had felt when he thought he had lost her.

"Andrews! This is my last warning!" Merced screamed.

Tap felt a soft, peaceful wind waft across the street. The tension around his eyes relaxed. He turned around and dragged Hager back toward Merced.

"What are you doin'?" Hager cried.

With Hager tugging him back to the west, Tap raised his Colt and pointed it toward Simp Merced's head. Merced's gun was still pointed at Andrews. The two men stood no more than ten feet apart in the middle of the intersection of 19th and Ransom Streets.

To the south, the loafers and bummers quieted as they stared into the street. The drovers on horseback on the north backed away. No one said a word. Above them the rolling clouds darkened the sky. The final click of the hammer on Tap's Colt cracked like a whip in the waiting silence.

"God help us. God help us! We're all dead men," Jerome Hager whimpered.

"Merced, shove that gun in your holster and get out of the street!" Tap was surprised at the calmness of his own voice. He didn't take his eyes off Merced.

"Wh-what?"

"Get off the street. You're a disgrace to everything Pappy stood for!"

"I've got a gun on you, Andrews!" Merced hollered in an extra loud voice. Sweat beaded the trembling man's forehead.

"Get off the street. . . . NOW!" Tap repeated in the same calm but commanding tone.

For nearly thirty seconds both men stood still and held cocked revolvers at each other.

Suddenly Simp Merced released the hammer of his revolver and shoved it into his holster. He hurried down the street to the east.

Tap prodded Jerome to resume walking toward the courthouse.

"You're crazy, Deputy! You almost started a war back there."

"Isn't it a beautiful day, Jerome?"

"What?"

"Did you feel that warm, sweet-flower breeze?"

"That wind's colder than a snowmelt stream. What are you talking about?" Hager mumbled.

Thanks, Lord.

Suddenly Tap felt the temperature drop.

And his eyes once again grew tense.

5

The "Magic City of the Plains" is perched at 6,062 feet elevation. But it's not in the mountains. Except for Crow Creek meandering through town, Cheyenne is basically flat.

Yet to Tap Andrews, the last two blocks to the courthouse felt like a steep uphill climb. The stiff, cold wind was in his face. Two mobs of angry men were at his back. Mingled among the sounds of hoofbeats and jingling spurs were oaths and curses and threats of impending violence.

"Don't turn around and don't slow down, Jerome."

"You ain't got to worry about me, Deputy. I never was so cheerful to see a courthouse in my life. Where are them soldier boys you promised?"

"I'm sure they'll be along shortly." Tap could feel the heavy, cold steel of the shackle on his left wrist and the polished walnut handle of the .44 Colt in his right hand.

When they reached the corner of Ferguson and 19th, the boardwalks were jammed with onlookers. No longer was it merely the armed camps of drovers and bummers that followed behind, but shopkeepers, railroad workers, schoolchildren, families, and clergymen. Mothers hid their children's faces in the folds of long, dark dresses. Short people stood on packing crates, and two dozen Chinese took a position on top of the jewelry store.

"You said we're jist goin' to sneak up to the courthouse!" Hager protested. "You surely don't know how to keep a secret, Deputy. Where did all these folks come from?"

"Hager, maybe the Lord sent 'em."

"How do you figure?"

"The more witnesses, the less chance of you or me gettin' bush-whacked."

"Don't reckon I ever thought of it that way."

"No . . . I don't expect you have."

There were no soldiers waiting at the courthouse. Besides a bat-tery of bundled-up, gawking court employees, the only others waiting for Tap were Baltimore Gomez and Carbine Williams. Baltimore stood on the granite steps of the courthouse cradling a '79 side-by-side 10-bore with twenty-inch barrels in his arm—and a big smile on his round, dark face.

"Takin' a quiet stroll, are you, Tap?"

"He's crazy!" Hager complained. "I'm chained up to a crazy man!"

"It didn't exactly turn out like I figured," Tap admitted. "Is the judge inside?"

"Yep. Him and a couple of lawyers."

"Have you seen any sign of some troops from Ft. Russell?" Tap pushed the tip of his hat back with the barrel of his drawn .44.

"Nope."

"Well, I'll take Jerome before the judge."

Baltimore motioned toward Carbine on the roof. "What do you want us to do?"

"Don't let anyone else come into the courthouse." Tap started to walk through the doors. Then he leaned back toward Baltimore. "Shoot above their heads. I don't want anyone hurt—especially you and Carbine."

Jerome Hager demanded a jury trial, and Judge J. A. Blair set a trial date of May 12. Hager was sentenced to be held in the guardhouse at Ft. Russell until the trial began or until the marshal or acting marshal determined it was safe to return him to the county jail.

Toward the end of the half-hour proceedings, Tap heard a com-motion in the back of the courtroom. A blue-caped lieutenant and six heavily armed soldiers entered and stood near the door.

I hope they brought more than six!

After the proceedings, Andrews delivered the prisoner to Lt. Morris T. Jackson. Tap reached into his coat pocket and pulled out a key to unlock the irons.

"Keep him safe for us, Lieutenant. We want to see old Jerome get a nice trial and a legal hanging."

Hager watched as Andrews unhooked the irons. "I thought you told that mob you didn't have a key!"

"I lied."

"But . . . ," Hager muttered.

"I told you I wasn't a deacon. If they thought they could have gotten you unlocked . . . well, there's no telling where you would be." Then Tap turned to the army officer. "How many men did you bring with you?"

"Step on out and check for yourself."

Andrews led the procession out of the courtroom to find an army ambulance parked in the street with a dozen mounted cavalrymen in front and another dozen waiting behind.

"That ought to do it—don't you think so, Jerome?"

"Makes a fella feel mighty important."

The lieutenant marched Jerome Hager to the van and loaded him into the back with the six soldiers. "We don't always have a contingent this size available for such duty, but Marshal Divide always treated us square when the boys came to town. They appreciated that. We'll take good care of him. But the word on the street is that it only took one deputy to bring him to the courthouse from across town."

"One deputy and divine providence," Andrews added. "Do you want me to ride along?"

"Only if you have nothing else to do."

"I need to stick around for Pappy's funeral."

"Anytime you need to come out and talk to the prisoner, you are more than welcome."

"According to my wife, I'm supposed to come out tomorrow night for some kind of a dance."

"Oh, the Calico Hop. Yes, sir, it will be a fine time. Hate to see them pull out."

"Who?"

"The Seventh Infantry. They're getting moved north. That's why we're having the dance. Hope to see you there."

"I reckon I don't have any other option. My wife's a very persuasive woman."

The crowd in the street around the courthouse dispersed in the cold spring air as the soldiers led the ambulance down 19th Street. Only a couple riders from the earlier mob followed the soldiers at a safe distance.

Lord, it's in Your hands. I've done what I could.

"Well, Tap . . . where do you need us now?"

Carbine Williams and Baltimore Gomez sauntered up behind him. As always Carbine needed a haircut and Baltimore a shave.

"Go home for dinner, and I'll meet you at Pappy's funeral. I imagine most of the town will be there."

"Who will watch the town if we're all out at the grave site?" Baltimore asked.

"We'll just have to figure nothin'll happen for that hour." Tap shrugged.

Baltimore cleared his throat. "I hope this don't sound disrespectful, Tap . . . but me and funerals don't mix. I don't like 'em—never have. I don't aim to go to this one. You know how much I respected Pappy. That ain't it at all. There's just somethin' about a funeral that causes me to break out in a terrible itch."

"I know what you mean," Carbine sympathized.

"You do?"

"Yep. I feel the same way about weddin's—especially my own!"

"What do you say, Tap? If you told me I had to stay downtown or at the jail, then I could beg out of the funeral."

"Baltimore, in my role as temporary acting marshal, I hereby assign you to keep an eye on 16th Street and the tracks this afternoon."

"Well," Gomez drawled, "I surely hate to miss Pappy's last doin's, but a man's got to do his job. Thanks, Tap. It'll sure help me to know what to say to Savannah next time I see her on the street."

"How's she doin'?" Carbine inquired, the smoke from his quirley lingering like gun smoke in front of him.

"Pepper reports her as strong as ever . . . but I figure it'll all crash down on her one of these days. There's only so much sorrow a person can pack around. I'm headin' over to check on 'em now."

"It's a wonder we didn't see 'em in this crowd. I ain't seen that many in the streets since that Italian led the two elephants down 16th Street. Pepper and Savannah must have been the only ones in town that didn't see you march Hager up to the courthouse."

Tap fastened the top buttons on his coat and jammed his hands into his pockets. "I'm surely glad it's over. Maybe town will settle down now. With the snow meltin' in the Black Hills and the crews pullin' out for the spring roundup, Cheyenne should start to empty out."

"It's been a long winter in that respect," Williams concurred.

Tap trotted Brownie down Ferguson toward the Inter Ocean Hotel. He found Pepper and Savannah eating dinner at a table next to a front window in the hotel dining room. Both women were trimmed out in black. A large, pink-vased rose decorated the white lace tablecloth.

"Ladies, do you mind if a deputy joins you for dinner?"

"Mr. Andrews, how delightful! It will be our pleasure. I believe you've met my companion, Mrs. Andrews?" Savannah teased.

"Yes, we've met." He grinned at his beaming wife. "But we don't often see each other, do we, ma'am?"

Pepper leaned over and kissed him on the cheek.

"What was that for?"

"That's because I miss you," she announced. "And, besides, the whole town is talking about how you brought in Hager and stood down both the bummers and the drovers. Frankly, I thought you were magnificent."

"You saw it?"

"Mr. Andrews, I believe everyone in the town witnessed your bravery," Savannah responded.

"I should have never got myself in such a scrape. I guess the Lord had mercy on me."

"And me as well," Pepper added.

"Mr. Andrews, your Pepper is a dear jewel. Frankly, I don't know how a driftin' lawman like yourself ever snagged such a treasure."

"Snagged her? Didn't Pepper ever tell you how she trapped me?" Tap waved at a waiter to bring him some coffee.

Savannah glanced up. "Trapped you?"

Pepper pushed away from the table. "I did what? You ensnared me, Mr. Tapadera Andrews, and you know it!"

"Well," Savannah drawled, "this does sound interesting!"

"I guess the truth of the matter is that we lied, deceived, and misled each other. But once we got hooked on each other . . . well, we sort of liked it," Tap tried to explain.

"Well, Mr. and Mrs. Andrews, I do believe you two will have to illuminate that as we eat."

"Oh, not today, Savannah," Pepper protested. "You've got the funeral to think about and—"

"That's precisely why I insist you tell me this juicy story! Nothing will help me more than getting my mind off the service."

It took forty minutes, a bowl of pork stew, one small loaf of bread, and three cups of coffee before Tap and Pepper finished explaining the beginning of their relationship. Savannah Divide just laughed and shook her head.

Then both women excused themselves and retired to Suite G while Tap sat at the table and stared out the front window. Broken sunlight sprayed through the clouds.

I'll still need my overcoat. Standin' at the grave site of a friend has got to be the coldest spot on earth.

The voice was deep, unfamiliar, and obviously very excited. "Now here's the beauty of it. She sold it for only one dollar. Can you imagine what this will fetch in Boston or New York?"

Tap continued to stare out the window but listened intently to the conversation at the table next to him.

"You could probably sell it for twenty-five dollars!" This was a higher-pitched male voice.

"Twenty-five? Look at this signature. . . . It's Jesse's all right. I saw his name one time on a hotel registry in St. Joe. This is the authentic thing!"

Tap turned back to view the two men. Both wore tight suits, starched shirts, and dark ties.

"How did you say you came across it?" the smaller man with a receding hairline inquired.

"Well, this young lady, a girl actually, eh, like I said, she's Bob Ford's niece. I guess the family's in hard straits out here. You know, lots of folks consider Ford the villain in the story. Anyway, she was right at the ticket counter, crying her eyes out because she didn't have enough money to go to St. Joseph."

"And you offered to help her?"

"No, I didn't think about it until she tugged on my sleeve and wanted to know if I would buy her shoes for a dollar."

"Shoes?"

"Well, I wasn't about to buy a little girl's only pair of shoes. Then she pulled out this reward poster. She said it was the only thing of value she had, but she didn't know if it was worth a dollar."

"A dollar? You got a steal, Leo."

"That's what I figured. Look at this . . . '$25,000 reward, dead or alive.' Signed by the St. Louis-Midland Railroad. And right there—look at it: 'Your pal, Jesse James.' A genuine autograph."

Tap strolled over near the table.

"Excuse me, I just overheard a little of the conversation. Did you happen to get that wanted poster from a ten-year-old girl with coal-black curly hair, dark skin, dancing eyes, and a turned-up nose?"

"Yes, yes. That's her. Do you know her?"

"Yep."

"Listen, I know her last name's Ford, but what's her first name?" the man asked.

"Angelita." Tap sighed. "Her name is Angelita."

He rode Brownie down by the U. P. Station but didn't spot Angelita anywhere. He stopped at the mayor's hotel to talk about what to do with Simp Merced. Tom Breshnan was still gone, so he rode back to the house and changed into his Sunday suit. After washing his neck and shaving, he took one last look in the mirror.

His brown eyes looked strained. A streak of gray could be seen in the hair above his left ear, and the bruise on the side of his neck was turning yellow.

I will never, ever get used to wearin' these clothes. It's not natural. A man wasn't created to strut around all slicked up like this. If we had that ranch in the hills, I wouldn't have to . . . except for church and funerals, I suppose.

Stepping out to the front porch, Tap glanced across the street. Someone peeked out from the Wallace home. He tipped his hat and nodded. The curtains ruffled shut.

If there was anyone in Cheyenne besides Baltimore Gomez who didn't attend Pappy Divide's funeral, Tap couldn't tell it. Wrapped in topcoats, cloaks, and assorted wool blankets, the city gathered under heavy, gray clouds to hear Rev. H. H. Dixon shout the service. A cannon brought in from Ft. Russell sounded the farewell tribute. After a few words with Pepper and Savannah, Tap led Pappy's buckskin saddle horse back to the I-X-L Livery. Willie Templeton met him at the barn to collect the animals.

"Shore do seem strange not to have Pappy ridin' ol' Pancake, don't it?"

"Yep. This town will miss him."

"I don't figure how he got it," Willie continued. "He's the one man in town who seemed to get along with ever'one."

"All it takes is one blurry-eyed drunk. It could have been any of us."

"Yes, sir, Deputy. You're right about that. We're all livin' on borrowed time, so to speak. It'll take a good spell to find someone who can take Pappy's place."

"Willie, Pepper and I will be goin' out to the Fort tomorrow evening. You got a buggy we can rent?"

"You invited to that Calico Hop?"

"That's what I hear."

"Well, I'll be. . . . I reckon I didn't figure you for the dancin' type. You want a standard or deluxe carriage?"

Tap pulled his rifle out of his scabbard and walked to the barn door. "I want the cheap one, Willie. The cheap one."

Later that evening he sat at the kitchen table cleaning his guns by the flickering light of a poorly trimmed lantern.

I can't believe I told Pepper to spend another night with Savannah. We've only been married three months, but a man sure does get used to having a woman at home every night. Lord, the whole thing sort of snuck up on me. I figured for years that I just wasn't the religious type. Then . . . all of a sudden there You were staring me down out of the pages of Hatcher's Bible.

And I just knew I wasn't the marrying kind. But Pepper comes along, and I can't imagine not bein' married. Seems like You've been makin' a habit out of provin' me wrong—which is surely okay by me.

Holding a piece of white paper inside the receiver of the '73 Winchester to reflect the lantern's light, Tap looked down the barrel of the rifle and nodded approval of the bore. Placing the cleaning tools back in the oily leather sack, he pumped ten shells into the rifle and set it by the front door.

Then he loaded his .44 Colt with five rounds and carried it and the lantern to the bedroom. Within minutes he had stripped down to his long johns and slipped underneath the covers. He reached over to the right side of the bed and laid his hand across Pepper's lilac-smelling pillow.

I just can't believe I let her stay at Savannah's!

Aimee "Pepper" Paige Andrews stood robe-wrapped and stared out the front window of Suite G at the Inter Ocean Hotel. Cheyenne's new incandescent street lights were a marvel to look at. But the real reason she couldn't sleep was the weeping she heard coming from Savannah's room.

Lord, I just don't know what else to say . . . what else to do!

I'm not very good at this. I don't know very much. Help her, Lord. Ease the pain in her heart. I need her to be strong. We all need Savannah to be strong!

I miss Tap, Lord. I wish I was home. I never thought I'd get used to being married so quickly. He looked so tired at the funeral today. He needs the rest. He's probably been asleep for hours. It's probably better that I'm not there to bother him.

She shuffled back over to her bed near the high-backed velvet sofa. Slipping off the robe, she climbed under the covers and pulled the flannel sheet up to her chin.

He's the only man on earth I've ever missed.

What am I doing here, Lord?

I want to go home!

Some aromas touch your memory and allow you to relive your past . . . good and bad. The smell of lupine always reminded Tap of his childhood—playing in the foothills of the great Sierra Nevadas along the Tuolumne River. The sweet, pungent aroma of vanilla incense brought him back to the fan-tan game on Sacramento Street in San Francisco and the first time he witnessed a man shot to death, when he was only sixteen. The smell of burnt hair coursed him back to the Santa Rosa Mountains and ten straight days of branding cattle for the Eight Slash Eight. Then there was the smell of the night-blooming cactus flower—deep, haunting, soaking in down to his bones. That reminded him of Teresa and the softest rabbit blanket in the world.

But for Tap there was no smell better than bacon frying on a cold morning. The aroma always sizzled and popped and beckoned him to another day. It shouted out, "Get up! There's a busy, adventuresome day waiting!" It seemed to make his toes wiggle, his mind awaken, and his tongue water.

He sat straight up in bed and pitched the covers to the cold wooden floor. Grabbing his hat and his holster in his left hand, he shuffled out to the kitchen. He blinked his eyes at the apparition hovering over the cookstove.

"Pepper? Darlin', what in the world are you doin' here?"

"I live here . . . remember? Surely I haven't been gone that long!"

"But—but I thought . . . Didn't you stay at Savannah's?"

"Yes. Now are you going outside dressed like that? Or do you have time for some bacon and eggs?"

"Oh, well . . . I, eh, you know . . . didn't know you were out here."

"Obviously."

He stepped over and slipped his arms around her and kissed the back of her neck. "I'm glad you're home."

"So you missed me?" She tried to brush her hair back off her face.

"Pepper, I laid awake most of the night wonderin' if I ought to sneak over to the hotel and pirate you off in your sleep."

"It wouldn't have worked."

"Why not?"

"I wasn't asleep. Now go pull on some britches and let's eat breakfast. Has Mrs. Wallace been keeping a good eye on you?"

"Like a hawk."

"Have you got a busy day planned?"

"Well, we're goin' to be shorthanded. I'm goin' to make sure Merced is fired today. There's no way to work with a man who gives in to a lynch mob."

"I hear Mr. Merced has a number of friends around town, especially down at DelGatto's."

"Good. He shouldn't have any trouble finding another job."

About 7:00 A.M. they finished breakfast.

Tap didn't make it to the marshal's office until almost nine.

To his surprise the sky was clear. The south wind had completely blown away all the clouds of the previous day. The breeze felt cool, but not cold, and the hint of spring was strong in the songs of the birds and the swell of the cottonwood buds. Even the winter gloom that yesterday had depressed his spirit seemed lifted and replaced with a hope generated from a much deeper source than merely the weather.

Carbine Williams, shaggy black hair curling out from under his hat, stood at the hall door talking to someone in the jail cells.

"Mornin', Tap." Carbine nodded. "We figured you might be takin' the day off."

"No, it's just that . . . I was, you know, a little bushed and . . . Who do you have locked up this morning?"

"Just LaPorte, McKay, and a sleepin' drover."

"Mornin', boys!" Tap called.

"Deputy, please don't shout so loud," a weak voice filtered in from the cells.

"Have you seen Merced?"

"Nope. Maybe he went into hiding after you stood him down in the street."

"I want his badge and his keys. We're all in this job together, and we can't have one goin' off on his own like that."

"I'll tell him," Carbine replied, "but I don't think he'll listen to anyone but the city council."

"They'll be meetin' in the next day or two. In the meantime . . . well, I'll tell Simp myself." Tap sorted through a stack of papers piled on the desk.

Carbine swung open the front door. He reached into the pockets of his gray wool vest, took out his makings, and began to roll a smoke. "Sure does feel good to have Hager out at the Fort and spring in the air. You reckon town will calm down now?"

"I surely hope so. But I got a feelin' in my gut that Hager isn't the only source of contention around here. Anyway . . . maybe I'm wrong. Listen, can you and Baltimore handle things this evenin'? Pepper and I have to—"

"You goin' to that Calico Hop?"

"Eh, yeah, it's sort of a tradition for the marshal to—"

"Well, don't that beat all. I bet Angelita two bits you and Pepper weren't the dancin' kind."

"I never was too good," Tap admitted with a wry grin, "but Pepper can dance the boots off that entire Fort. So I'll go out and stumble around a bit."

"Don't y'all worry about nothin'. With Hager out of town and good weather comin' on, the drovers will be pullin' out to the roundup, and the rest of the bummers will be wanderin' on up to the Black Hills."

"That's surely what I'm hopin'. Carbine, you haven't seen Angelita, have you?"

"Reckon she's down at the U. P. The westbound ought to be rollin' in soon. She ain't sellin' minin' stock again, is she?"

"No. Looks like she's got a new scheme. Tell Simp I want to see him if he happens to show his head."

Tap walked down Ferguson Street, cut over on 16th, and headed for the Union Pacific Station. The terminal was filled with people waiting for the train's arrival. Several times a week the Denver train and the east/west train rolled in at the same time. The depot was always crowded. He skirted around the crowd and stacks of baggage, but he couldn't spot Angelita. Finally, he plopped down on a back bench and pulled his hat low over his eyes. He purposely tugged his canvas coat over the deputy badge that decorated his vest. Stretching his legs out in front of him, he closed his eyes and waited.

Steel clanged and steam hissed as the train pulled in. The terminal buzzed with noise, but above it all Tap heard the plaintive, weeping voice of a small, frightened girl.

"And if I don't have the twenty dollars by noon, they said they would kick grandmother out of the hospital."

"You say they belonged to Wild Bill Hickok?"

"Yes, sir. These is the very cards he was holdin' when that villain Jack McCall shot him in the back of the head up at Carl Mann's #10 Saloon in Deadwood. My daddy was sittin' at the table that day—August 2, 1876. And I promised on his dyin' bed I'd never sell these cards . . . but," she sobbed, "Grandma is all I have left. If she doesn't get well, I don't know what I'll do."

The wailing continued.

A woman's voice interjected, "Millard, give the little girl some money!"

"But twenty dollars for black aces and eights—"

"And a jack."

"It seems rather steep even if it were authentic. Besides, how do we know . . ."

The crying had now almost silenced the entire crowd at the terminal.

"Millard, everyone is staring!" the woman insisted.

"Mister, you won't go wrong with this purchase. A man down at the Front Range Club in Denver offered Daddy over one hundred dollars for these cards. He said he would post them behind the bar."

"But really I just can't—"

"You're going to Denver on the spur, aren't you?"

"Yes, but—"

"Take them to the Front Range Club and sell 'em. I'd do it myself, but I don't have the fare, and I can't leave my grandma. Please, mister," she whimpered.

"Millard!"

"Oh . . . all right. But it's against my better judgment." The man began to reach into the pocket of his tailored suit.

"Angelita!" Tap called out as he stood up and walked toward her.

She spun around on the heels of her black lace-up boots and shouted, "Uncle Tap! Uncle Tap! Where have you been?"

As he walked toward the startled couple, Angelita leaped into his arms, throwing her arms around his neck.

"You cost me twenty dollars," she whispered through a cheesy smile.

"I've just stopped by to see your grandmother," Tap reported. "I paid the bill, so you don't have to sell the family heirloom."

"You did?" she beamed. Then she muttered under her breath, "You jerk!"

"Yes, and she's feeling much better and calling for you. You'd better run along now."

"Oh, yes, Uncle Tap! Isn't this wonderful news!" She waved at the bewildered couple. Stuffing the cards back into a pocket in her dress, she scampered toward the door.

"I'll talk to you later, Uncle Tap!" she hollered.

"Yes, you will," he replied.

"My, she is quite a spirited young lady. You must be proud of her determination and ingenuity," the woman observed.

"Well . . . she is quite a gal, all right."

"So," the man interjected, "that really was Wild Bill's last hand? I almost had it for twenty dollars! I can't believe it! Wait until I tell my friends back in Philadelphia. They won't believe it!"

"Yeah, it's unbelievable, all right. Hope you folks have a nice trip to Denver."

"Thank you, Mr. . . . ."

"Andrews. Tap Andrews."

After a quick lunch with Pepper, Tap spent most of the afternoon poking his head into places like Braun's Saloon, Bescherer's Restaurant, C. G. Strom's, Smith & Harrington's, the Railroad Hotel, Ramsey's Restaurant, Goldaker's Barber Shop and Bathing Rooms, Justus & Ahrens' Saloon, Fred Landau's Billiard Parlor, and John Geer's Tobacco Shop, looking for Simp Merced. Although many folks reported seeing Simp during the day, Tap was unable to locate him. Tap was just crossing 16th Street when a young voice filtered down from an open second-story window.

"You owe me twenty dollars, Mr. Tapadera Andrews!"

"Angelita, what are you doin' up there?"

"I'm baby-sitting for Mrs. Clayton."

"Good. You ought to do more of that."

"For twenty-five cents?"

"What?"

"I get twenty-five cents for three hours. What kind of deal is that? You owe me twenty dollars."

"The judge would have given you a twenty-dollar fine for swindling passengers on the U. P."

"Swindle? How do you know those weren't Hickok's cards?"

"Because yours have numeral digits on them. Hickok's didn't."

Angelita stuck out her tongue and ducked back behind the curtains.

"Fun for the Boys at Cowhick and Witcomb's." Tap stood on the boardwalk reading the advertising sign in the front window

of the men's clothing store. *"Done with high prices! Fine clothing cheap! No old goods. All new!"*

"Deputy," a big-bellied clerk called from the front door, "we've got a good assortment of wool suits for only twelve dollars."

"I've got one suit. What would I do with two? I was just thinkin' about a tie," Tap explained.

"Oh, come in and see our fine assortment of silk ties. They're only fifty cents. There are some fancy flowered ones direct from Paris."

"Mister, can you even imagine me wearin' somethin' like that?"

"Eh . . . no, sir, I don't suppose I could."

"Neither can I!" Tap tipped his hat and scooted across the street in front of a slow-moving freight wagon.

Tap didn't bother explaining to Pepper how uncomfortable he felt in the white starched shirt and the breath-cheating tie. She was spinning around the house in a whirl of giggles, songs, and dances.

"You look mighty happy, Mrs. Andrews."

"And you look terribly handsome, Mr. Andrews. Isn't this dress wonderful? I had no idea that Savannah and I were so close to the same size! She's a little bigger in the . . . well, you know, but not much. Really it fits well, don't you think? Do you like the cap? The color looks ravishing on her, but I think it's fairly passable on me. What do you think? I mean, provided my hair will stay back in the combs. Which it never does, does it?"

"Eh, well . . ."

"Oh, Tap, we haven't been dancing since . . . Actually it's about the first time I've gone to a dance where the men aren't paying me. I like it. I thought I never wanted to dance again. I told you that, remember? But now it seems so . . . well, so sociable. Isn't it going to be a grand evening?"

"Yep, I reckon it—"

"Honey, could you help me with my boots? I feel a little dizzy," Pepper admitted. "Maybe I should sit down for a minute."

"You've been spinning around this house for two hours. Let me . . ."

"I guess I'm a little nervous. Are you? Of course, you aren't. You're never nervous. Good, old, steady Tap. You were a little nervous at the wedding though. I think it's the only time I've ever seen you nervous. Remember how you fell and got your shirt muddy? Oh, my . . . is it a little warm in here? If I don't get some fresh air, I believe I'll faint."

"I stoked up the fire so it would last until we get home. What time do you figure we'll be—"

"You know, Tap, in some ways this is one of our first real important social events. I mean, I know it's not a ball over at the Sturgis home or something like that. But for us, it's a very important event. Do you think they'll like me?"

"You'll turn every man's head in the building. I think you're—"

"Oh, no, no, no. I didn't mean the men. Goodness, who cares about the men? I mean the wives. Do you think the wives will think I'm . . . you know, charming and witty and good company but not threatening?"

"Darlin', I don't think you—"

"Will the mayor and his wife be there?"

"I heard they might not make it back today. Their eldest daughter is still down in that Denver sanatorium and—"

"Well, how about the council members? And Judge and Mrs. Carey? And the Whitcombs?"

"Actually I did hear that—"

"She's a Sioux, I hear. I knew she was dark, but, my, you'd never know it by those children. I don't think there's a finer family in this town! You should hear how respectful they are to guests."

"Where did you learn all—"

"Savannah knows everything. She will really miss going to the hop. I think it would be good for her to go visit her sister in Charleston. I mean, it would take her mind off everything. What do you think? Tie it a little tighter. What do you think, Tap?"

"About your shoe?"

"No. About Savannah going to Charleston to visit her sister?"

"I don't know about Savannah, but I can tell you something about Mrs. Andrews."

"What's that?"

"You're about as anxious as a hen layin' her first egg."

"I am not!" She swung to her feet and tucked her hands on her blue-calico-draped hips. "This is certainly not the first dance I've ever gone to! Oh, my!"

"What's the matter?"

"Oh, I guess having a late supper like this makes me dizzy."

"Well," Tap inserted, "if you don't feel like goin', I'm sure I could—"

"Mr. Andrews, you are going to drive me out to Ft. Russell in that rented carriage, and we will have a delightful time at the Calico Hop. Do you understand?"

"Yes, ma'am." He winked and shoved on his new black hat.

6

THE CHEYENNE DAILY LEADER, *Wednesday, April 4, 1883.*

FORT RUSSELL. *A Calico Hop was given at the post last evening, which proved a great success. There were at least ninety couples, the ladies being attired in various pretty calico gowns and caps that made them look quaint and picturesque. There were many handsome, young ladies there. Mrs. Tapadera Andrews was pronounced "Belle of the Ball." Miss Laura Hardin and Miss Nancy Gregory, as well as several officers and their wives from Fort Laramie, also attended.*

As this was a farewell ball for the Seventh Infantry, the program was varied. The Russell Specialty Company gave a concert, singing selections between each dance, which were highly enjoyed by all. Al Lewis, Lou Kortmann, and Will Jameson sang some very pleasing selections.

Coronation of the "Belle" took place at midnight with the selection of Cheyenne's own Pepper Andrews being nearly unanimous. It was rumored that Mrs. Andrews spent several years studying dance in New York City. According to all accounts, her ability demonstrated last evening confirms that speculation.

At eleven o'clock Tap plopped down on a bench at the back of the hall, loosened his tie, and unfastened his collar. His feet hurt. His knees hurt. His arms hurt.

For the next hour he tried to stay awake as he watched Pepper dance with every officer and gentleman in the room. By the time she was voted "Belle of the Ball," Tap had to be awakened to learn the news. He stumbled through a final dance with Pepper. Then they adjourned to the waiting rented carriage.

"I can't believe you went to sleep on that bench!" she teased. "You didn't even get to vote."

"Was the voting close?" he asked, as he turned his coat collar up and stretched a lap blanket across them.

"Well, not really," she pouted, "but you didn't vote for me."

"I vote for you every day of the year," Tap chided. "Darlin', you danced the shoes off those army boys. You had fun, didn't you?"

"Do you know what I like?" Pepper rubbed her gloved hands to warm them. "They all treated me so nice. No vulgar language. No improper touches. No propositions. You know, I think I like having a husband who wears a badge and a gun!" She slipped her arm in his and laid her head on his shoulder as the carriage rolled along the three-mile road to Cheyenne. The stars hung low and bright. It was difficult for her to see where the night horizon ceased and the twinkling lights of Cheyenne began.

"You're not still feeling dizzy or sick, are you?" Tap's leather gloves felt cold and stiff.

"Oh, no. It seemed like once I got to the ballroom, I felt terrific. You wouldn't believe how many ladies asked me how I learned to dance so well."

Tap rubbed the back of his neck and tried stretching the stiffness out of it. "Well, darlin', what did you tell them?"

"I just said it took years and years of practice. That was all right, wasn't it? I didn't lie. But I really didn't want to tell them about the dance halls and all that." She pulled the hood of her cape over her calico cap.

"Pepper girl, that's the beauty of God's forgiveness. We get to start over again. I keep tellin' you, folks around here don't care what you were. They only look at what you are—right now."

"Will you take me to another ball sometime?" she purred as she kissed his cold ear.

"Sure. Just give me six months to rest up. Mrs. Andrews, you ought to live in one of those big houses on Ferguson Street and have your own ballroom."

"Only if my Tap is there with me. Did I ever tell you I actually like being married to you?"

"I think you might have mentioned it a time or two." He reached over and slipped his arm around her shoulders and held her close—all the way home.

Pepper was fast asleep by the time they reached the outskirts of Cheyenne. The road smoothed out, and there was no sound but the clomp of the horses' hooves and the squeak of the carriage wheels. Instead of driving down 17th to the livery, Tap swung the carriage over by the Union Pacific tracks.

Might as well see if everything's under control in the hurdy-gurdies. Carbine can keep 'em quiet as long as no one calls him a half-breed. He and Baltimore are steady as rocks. A man could go to the bunk on their support. I guess two out of three isn't too bad. Simp shouldn't be a lawman—he's all bluff and no show. You can't let a mob push you one inch. He'll do all right bouncin' at DelGatto's, runnin' errands for the big boys, ridin' shotgun on the stage. Maybe he's just in over his head and can't figure it out. In the long run, I'm doin' him a favor.

"Tap! Tap, is that you? Wait up!" Someone carrying a rifle and waving his hat ran through the night toward their carriage.

Andrews's left hand held the reins tight, and his right hand had drawn the Colt .44. He waved the revolver in the dark toward the sound of the voice.

"Carbine?"

"Tap . . . Evenin', Mrs. Andrews." Carbine Williams tipped his hat toward the reclining Pepper.

"I think she's asleep," Tap whispered.

"Just as well." Williams waited for two men on horseback to ride past them.

"What's the matter, Carbine? We got trouble?"

"Not we. You."

Andrews swung down off the carriage. "What do you mean?" The night noises seemed hushed, and he couldn't see anyone else on the street.

"Have you seen Simp Merced yet?"

"No. Is he looking for me? He didn't get soused and call me out, did he?"

"It's worse than that, Tap. You ain't talked to Nagle or Whipple?"

"The councilmen? No. We're just comin' back from that dance at Ft. Russell. Why? Do they want to see me?"

"They was the ones selected to tell you."

"Tell me what?"

"Eh . . . Tap, I'm jist goin' to come right out with it, okay?"

"Carbine, what's this all about?"

"They had a council meetin' tonight."

"Tonight? I thought the mayor was out of town."

"He is, but they called an emergency meeting."

"And nobody remembered to tell me?"

"I guess you was the subject of the discussion."

"You mean the appointment of an interim marshal?"

"Tap, here's the facts as Nagle and Whipple explained to me and Baltimore. Some folks showed up at the meetin' complainin' about you. So the council has suspended you, with pay, until they finish investigatin' the charges."

"Charges? Against me? Is it about what happened in Arizona? That's all been cleared up."

"Don't know nothin' about Arizona. But they said you acted illegally in caching Hager at your house, thereby endangerin' the neighborhood. They said he should have been kept at the jail. Second, you needlessly jeopardized the safety of hundreds of citizens of Cheyenne by the theatrics of marching Hager through the city streets. You acted imprudently in allowing a child to escort the prisoner."

"A child?"

"Angelita, I reckon."

"Is this a joke?"

"And some felt you misused your temporary position by undermining the authority of a fellow deputy. I guess they mean when you backed Simp down."

"Did Merced put them up to this? He can't do this to me!"

"I reckon he, Alex DelGatto, and some of them other southsiders already did. The council appointed Merced acting marshal until an election can be held."

"They what? Merced! He couldn't marshal a prairie dog town!"

"Ain't that the truth!"

Tap slapped his hand down on the carriage seat in disgust. Pepper sat up and rubbed her eyes. "What happened? Where are we, honey? Did something fall apart?"

"This whole world is fallin' apart, darlin'."

"What?"

"Evenin', ma'am. I'm surely sorry to disturb you, but I couldn't let it ride 'til mornin'."

"What is it, Tap?"

"I got fired."

"No . . . really—what's happening?"

"The city fathers decided they didn't want me wearin' a badge."

"Did they find out about Arizona?" she asked.

"Nope."

"I don't even want to know what happened in Arizona," Carbine continued, "but me and Baltimore talked it over. We didn't want to leave the city unguarded at night, so we ain't quittin' until mornin'."

"No, you boys don't need to quit on account of me."

"We ain't quittin' on account of you. We don't trust Simp any further than we kin toss him. We don't want to work for him."

"I appreciate the thought, Carbine. But I'll get this thing straightened out as soon as the mayor gets back to town. So why don't you two hang in there a few more days. You can at least try to keep up some form of order."

"It ain't worth it, Tap. If that's the kind of law they want, let 'em have it."

"Work 'til payday at least," Tap encouraged him.

"I don't know. . . . I mean, I'll stay on tonight and talk it over with Baltimore in the mornin'."

"This is a big mistake. I'll get it straightened out. I've still got the marshal's badge."

"Yeah, but they want you to turn it in."

"What if I don't? Who they goin' to send to take it away from me? Simp can't do it."

"Me and Baltimore won't have anything to do with it either."

Tap shook his head. "This is crazy. Sort of like a bad dream."

"Go on home and git some sleep." Carbine looked up and down the deserted dirt street. "That council meetin' was about the only excitement in this town. Ever'thing's real quiet."

"I'll go home, but I don't figure I'll get much sleep."

He was right.

Tap and Pepper sat at the hardwood kitchen table drinking coffee from blue tin cups, talking until dawn.

With his marshal's badge crammed into his wool vest pocket, Tap pushed his way out of the house at about 6:30 A.M. Pepper was asleep on the bed still clothed in the new gingham dress when he left. He hadn't felt like eating. The morning clerk at Breshnan's said the mayor had arrived late the previous evening and would probably sleep in. Tap left a note asking him to look him up when he stirred around.

He started to walk up toward the marshal's office and then turned around. *I'm not in a real good mood to meet Simp Merced. Lord, I'm not in a real good mood to meet anyone! I'm not sure this deputy thing brings out the best in me.*

He wound up at the Drovers' Cafe with several cups of coffee and a bear sign. He was halfway through the third cup when

Angelita, wrapped in a white-speckled rabbit fur coat, climbed up on the bench beside him.

"Morning, Mr. Andrews. Sorry about you getting fired. Daddy told me you got a bum deal. Do you like my new coat?"

"It's beautiful, darlin'. Where did you get that?"

"I made an honest trade," she divulged. "I traded an old cap-and-ball pistol for it."

"Now you didn't tell them that it once belonged to Bill Hickok, did you?"

"Of course not!" Angelita bristled.

"Good."

"I told them the gun once belonged to Stuart Brannon."

"Angelita!"

"How do I know it didn't once belong to him?"

Tap shook his head and sighed. "You're goin' to get yourself in real trouble one of these days."

"Me? You're the one who got fired."

"Well, maybe I can get that straightened out this mornin'."

"I certainly hope so. Daddy's talking about quitting and moving on. He's thinking of us going on up to Deadwood. Have you ever been up there, Mr. Andrews?"

"Eh . . . not yet."

"Neither have I. And I don't want to go."

Suddenly Angelita climbed up on the stool and faced the dozen or so customers in the restaurant. "I am going to sing a song, and I'd like to dedicate this to Mr. Tapadera Andrews who just got fired from being a deputy even though everyone knows he's the bravest man in town. He's been a good friend to me although I sometimes act like a pill."

She locked her hands together in front of her and tilted her head slightly to the right.

"'The roundhouse in Cheyenne is filled every night
    With loafers and bummers of most every plight.
On their back is no clothes, in the pockets no bills;
    Each day they keep starting for the dreary Black Hills.
Don't go away; stay at home if you can;*

Stay away from that city, they call it Cheyenne,
Where the blue waters roll and the Comanche Bills
Will lift up your head in the dreary Black Hills.'"

Angelita vocalized the second and third verses. When she finished, there was a loud ovation. Several coins were tossed her way.

"Maybe I should be a singer when I grow up," she announced as she scooped up the coins and plopped down next to Tap.

"What makes you think you aren't grown up?"

"I'm buying your coffee and roll," she announced. "You'll need to save up all your money now that you don't have a job."

"All right, I'll let you buy them."

"You will? Really? Is it proper for a young lady to buy a married man his breakfast? You said I was nearly grown, right? I wouldn't think you would allow me to do something so indelicate."

Tap sighed and pulled a couple coins out of his gray wool vest pocket, stacking them on the counter. As he stood to leave, Hiram Porter came through the door.

"Tap . . . you got a minute?"

"What can I do for you?"

"I heard about your run-in with the city council. I'm pulling three wagons up to the roundup in Johnson County. Things are crazy up there. Rustlers and squatters all over the place. I'd like to hire you to oversee the range, just to make sure ever'one is playin' by the rules. I'll put you up and feed you and give you eighty dollars a month."

"Thanks, Mr. Porter. I'll surely consider it. When do you need to know?"

"Got to pull out Friday, no matter what the weather."

Tap received two more roundup job offers on his way back to the mayor's. So many stopped him to visit that it was after eleven before he made it to Breshnan's office.

"Well, Tap, it looks like I missed all the excitement," the mayor commented.

"Not necessarily. There might be more fireworks today."

"No . . . well, actually what I meant was that I missed seeing you bring in Jerome Hager."

"And you missed the council meeting." Tap glanced up at the wood-paneled wall that sported a large stuffed bull elk head.

"Yes, yes . . . I'm horribly sorry to have missed that meeting. I had no idea this was going to transpire."

"Can they legally do that? Can they hold a meeting without you being present and fire me?"

"As far as I can figure . . . without an elected marshal they can do that."

"Can't you reverse it?"

"I don't think so. I mean, not without dire political consequences. This is an election year, you know." The mayor shrugged. "Actually it might be a good thing."

"What are you talking about?"

"Hear me out, Tap. Alex DelGatto was the one who pushed this through. He's also the one who keeps threatening to run against me for mayor. I figure this blunder will sink his ship for good."

"Right at the moment I don't give a buffalo chip about your reelection chances."

"Oh . . . no, quite right. But the council will call for election of a marshal within the next six weeks. Lots of folks are upset about them sitting you down, and you'll be able to get their votes real easy. My opinion is that this council action just gave you the election."

"In the meantime, I don't have a job, and Merced is acting marshal during Jerome Hager's trial."

"I'll be happy to personally hire you for six weeks at the deputy's pay to work for me. As far as the trial is concerned, you've got Hager out at Ft. Russell, and Judge Blair is on top of the situation. I don't think you need to worry. I'll try to get the election set as quickly as possible. And you can certainly count on my endorsement."

Tap took deep breaths and tried to keep his anger from exploding.

"Now if you'll turn in the marshal's badge to me, I'll take care of the other details. Shall I put you on my payroll starting today?"

Tap stormed toward the door. "Breshnan, I'm not workin' for you, and if Merced wants the badge, tell him to come see me about it. I'm not surrenderin' Pappy's badge to any man too cowardly to come look me in the eye."

Tap walked briskly toward the I-X-L stables.

I didn't handle that good, Lord! Maybe You better keep Merced away from me for a while . . . and the city council and the mayor and . . .

Just before noon Tap drove the rig to the front of their house on 17th Street and bounded across the yard to the door. Mrs. Wallace was at her place behind the lace curtain.

Pepper sat at the piano bench beside the massive piano combing her hair.

"You goin' to play me a tune?" he teased.

"Sure. Are you going to sing me a song?"

Pepper patted the bench beside her, and Tap slid in next to her.

"Did you get any sleep?" he asked.

"A few hours. What did you find out?"

"They really fired me."

"I can't believe this! They can't fire a man for doing a good job. There isn't a man in this town who could have done what you did yesterday! Who do they think they are, hiding in those big mansions on Ferguson Street! You're the only man left in this town who can face down the whole lot of them, and they know it. I have a good mind—"

"Yes, you do," Tap interrupted. "And the rest ain't bad either. Now calm down, Mrs. Andrews. There's a carriage out there waitin' for you to pack us a picnic and go for a ride."

She spun her head so quickly that her blonde hair bounced off his face. "Really? Just you and me?"

Pulling back a little, Tap flashed a teasing smile. "Just the two of us."

"Where are we going?"

"Anyplace we can laugh, shout, holler, cry, complain, kiss, and cuss without it botherin' the neighbors."

"No cussing. I've already heard enough foul language to last a lifetime."

"Right. No cussing."

"Is it cold out?"

"It's pleasant and sunny now, but you know how it can change. We'd better take plenty of wraps."

Pepper buzzed through the house taking food out of the oven and gathering supplies. Tap loaded quilts into the carriage. He shoved his '73 Winchester under the buggy seat along with a box of shells. He had just toted the food box to the rig and returned to fetch Pepper when he noticed a tear slide down her face.

"You feelin' sick again, babe?"

"No." She sniffled.

"Darlin', you're cryin'. Hey, it's okay. I'll find another job. Maybe the Lord's tryin' to tell me somethin'. Maybe I'm just not cut out to be a—"

"It's not that," she whispered.

"Well, what is it?" Tap slipped his arm around her shoulder.

"This is the first time in my life I've ever gone on a picnic." She hung her head low.

"You're kiddin' me."

"No. It's my very first time."

"But . . . but what about when you were little—back in Georgia?"

"The war was on. Then they burned Atlanta . . . and daddy died."

"But what about up in Idaho? Your mother and her husband—didn't they . . ."

"Mama was always sick, Tap. And the others—they treated me mean. Real, real mean."

"But even dance-hall girls have time for picnics, don't they?"

"Nobody ever invited me on one." The tears now streamed freely down both sides of her cheeks.

Tap held her tight. "Well, you're goin' on a picnic today, girl, and I promise it won't be the last."

Pepper wiped her eyes with the hankie she had tucked into the sleeve of her yellow gingham dress and then followed him out to the rig. They were rambling east out of Cheyenne when she finally spoke. "Honey, I'm sorry I was so doleful back there. Every once in a while I remember how much I missed growin' up."

"Darlin, we've got a lifetime to make up for all you missed."

"I know it. It's not important. Maybe I am still feeling a little poorly. Your job is the important thing. It's so incredible I still can't believe it. Yesterday afternoon you could have been elected emperor of Cheyenne—and by nighttime they're firing you. I've never heard anything like it."

"Reminds ya a little of that crowd that shouted 'Hosanna!' one day and 'Crucify Him!' the next, doesn't it?" Tap suggested.

"I was thinking the same thing."

"You know what Pappy told me once?" Tap slapped the reins, and the team of driving horses broke into a trot on the outskirts of town. "He said, 'I don't trust crowds. Never have. Never will. Individual people matter, but the opinion of a crowd isn't worth a buffalo chip.'"

"Pappy just might be right. Now tell me everything the mayor said to you. Don't leave out a word."

"We can wait 'til we picnic to talk about that."

Pepper sat straight up and tilted her head in a schoolteacherly manner. "We will discuss what the mayor said right now, Mr. Andrews. I'm not about to waste the conversation on my first picnic on city politics. I've read about picnics. When we get there, we're going to talk about flowers and springtime and dances and concerts and good books we've read and poetry and . . . you know, things like that! Do you understand?"

"Yes, ma'am!" He grinned. "Say, do you know anything about poetry?"

"No. Do you?"

"Very little."

"That's all right. We'll just make something up, and neither of us will know the difference. Now tell me every word the mayor said."

He did.

Tap drove the carriage east along Crow Creek on the Campstool Road. Leaving the Union Pacific tracks to the north of them, they trotted along the rolling prairie of southeastern Wyoming. Near Rimer's corrals on the creek, they rested the horses. Tap carried the quilts and supplies from the carriage to a dry, grassy knoll that overlooked a southward bend in the creek.

"Are you too cold, darlin'?"

"Oh, no. I don't think it's nearly as windy as yesterday."

"Have you ever lived anyplace with more wind than Cheyenne?"

"Nope. Here. Put that crate down here. How about you?"

Tap spread the quilt on the grass and reclined while Pepper fussed through the supplies. A few white, puffy clouds sailed in the deep blue sky overhead. "You know," he sighed, "I don't guess I really lived anywhere—I mean, for any length of time in one location—before I met you. I sort of went season by season. A winter here . . . and spring there . . . and summer somewhere else."

"Should we build a fire and warm this food up?" Pepper pulled several biscuits out of a green-and-white-checkered napkin.

"Cold ham is fine with me, but I'll build you a fire if you need one."

"Well, if it clouds up, I might get cold."

"Listen, darlin'," Tap teased, "if you get cold, just scoot over here and let me warm you up."

"I've heard that line before." She shoved a large piece of biscuit and peach preserves into his mouth.

"Mnnnhppht."

"What did you say?"

"I said," he swallowed hard, "you seem to be takin' to this picnic thing mighty good."

"It's fun just to be away from the city and have you all to myself."

Tap opened a big biscuit, folded a piece of ham, and slapped it inside. "Did you ever think that maybe we'd be happier if we didn't live in a city like Cheyenne?"

Pepper wiped her mouth and motioned at him to open a jar of

applesauce. "You think it's time to move?" she finally managed to say.

"Oh, I don't know . . . this marshal thing—there's politics and different groups to make happy. And then you worry about justice and innocent people being falsely accused and guilty ones set free. Sometimes I get so mad I . . . well, sometimes I just figure I ought to shoot the whole lot of them."

"Tap!"

"Do you think I've been gettin' upset more since I've been deputyin'?"

"Hush, Mr. Andrews, we are not going to talk business. Besides, you are presently unemployed, so there's no reason to discuss it! Now I intend to talk poetry."

Tap laughed and gave her a squeeze. "All right, Mrs. Andrews—poetry it is. But you'll have to do all the talking. As I told you, I know very little rhymes."

"Not all poetry has to rhyme."

"See." He grinned. "I don't know very much about it."

"Well, Savannah let me borrow this book. I'll read you some."

"Can I keep eating while poetry is being read?"

"Certainly."

"Can I . . . you know, lay back and close my eyes?"

"In contemplation?"

"Of course."

"That's acceptable, but there will be a test after the reading, so you better not fall asleep."

"What if I just stretch out here and lay my head on this quilt."

"On my lap."

"What?"

"Haven't you ever read the books? You're supposed to stretch out and lay your head in my lap as I read the poetry and the warm spring breeze wafts through my golden locks."

"Are you kiddin'? I didn't know there were so many rules to follow!" Tap took a deep breath, tasting the freshness of early spring. "What is this warm breeze waftin' through your golden locks? Does the wind actually waft? You've been sittin' in Savannah's parlor too much."

"Quit complaining. I'm letting you off easy. You're supposed to be wearing a white shirt and tie and a silk top hat."

"I knew I didn't like poetry," he grumbled. He scooted over and laid his head in her lap. "Is this the proper way?"

"Yes, that will do nicely."

"Do I leave my eyes open or closed?"

"Whichever will help with your contemplation."

Tap closed his eyes. "Listen, is it acceptable for me to kiss the lady reading the poetry?"

"Certainly not!" Then her words turned into a giggle. "Not yet anyway. Now hush up and listen."

"Yes, ma'am." Tap scrunched around so that his holster and gun were more comfortable. Then he folded his hands on his stomach.

"I'll skip around to ones that . . . sort of make more sense than the others. Here's one . . . okay, here goes."

Tap waited, then opened his left eye. "Well?"

"I . . . uh . . . I've never read poetry out loud. Okay, I'm ready. Here goes."

"You said that before." He closed his eye.

> "'The year's at the spring
> And day's at the morn;
> Morning's at seven;
> The hillside's dew pearled;
> The lark's on the wing;
> The snail's on the thorn:
> God's in his heaven—
> All's right with the world!'"

Tap kept his eyes closed. "Robert Browning's *Pippa Passes*."

"How did you know that?" she pouted.

"Just a guess."

"I thought you said you didn't know anything about poetry!"

"I said I know very little about poetry. But this isn't my first picnic." He grinned and rolled to the side to avoid getting clobbered by his own hat that Pepper used as a swatter.

Tap scooted back over toward Pepper and put his head in her lap.
"Now don't interrupt me again," she scolded.
"I'll just contemplate silently."
"That would be nice."
Somewhere between the words: "'I sprang to the stirrup, and
Joris and he,'" and the couplet, "'I galloped, Dirck galloped, we
galloped all three,'" Tap fell asleep.

When he woke up, all the food had been neatly packed back
into the crate, but his head remained on Pepper's lap. The slight
breeze felt cooler, but Pepper's hand, running through his brown
hair, was warm.
"I think I was overcome with contemplation," he apologized.
Pepper smiled and laced his hand into hers. "It's all right. You
needed the rest."
Tap sat up and stretched his arms and legs. "But I haven't been
much company."
"I've had a delightful afternoon, Mr. Andrews. One of the
things I love best about being married is finding times when I can
sit and relax. I don't think I've seen you so relaxed . . . well, since
the company finally left after the wedding."
"You better enjoy all this quiet, Mrs. Andrews. When we start
having children, you'll keep busy enough."
She stared across the prairie for a while at the green grass just
starting to poke up out of the ground. "But the doctor said that I
probably couldn't have—"
"The doctor was wrong, and I don't want to talk about it!" Tap
stood to his feet and helped her up. "Now why don't we ride out
to Martin's ranch?"
"Can we get back to Cheyenne before dark?"
"Nope."
"But what about . . . I mean, where will we stay?"
"L. J.'s always wanting me to come out and see those Hereford
crosses of his. He said I can bunk with him."
"Bunking at a cattle ranch does not sound like—"
"How about curling up with me and some quilts in a hay loft?"

She raised her eyebrows. "That's a little better."

"Look, if I go back to town, I'll get angry over what's goin' on. This will give me more time to think."

"Well, then let's go to Martin's. He is married, isn't he?" She brushed out her dress with her hands.

Shoving on his new black hat, he began to fold the quilts. "Oh, ya, he's married. But Mrs. Martin spends a lot of time in New York City with her parents."

"Poor dear!" Pepper mimicked.

As they rolled east, the sun sank at their back, and the air chilled. They rattled and bumped along as Pepper held tightly to Tap's arm. By the time they reached the big stone house at the ranch, they had both quilts out and draped over their laps.

L. J. Martin's ranch stretched from the Texas trail to the big bend in Crow Creek. On rolling prairie and in grassy draws over 2,100 cows, calves, and bulls carried his brand. And it seemed to Pepper that she and Tap spent the better part of the next morning looking at every single bovine.

After an elegant noon meal prepared by a white-aproned chef and served on English china on a starched linen tablecloth, she and Tap departed for the long drive back to Cheyenne.

"You get enough to eat?" Tap asked as they rolled out of the stone and iron gate.

"Are you joking? I don't even know the names of some of those dishes."

"That oyster cream sauce was mighty savory."

"Yes. Thanks for showing me how to eat those green things."

Tap pulled down the brim of his hat. "The artichokes?"

"Yes. I thought they were part of the centerpiece. Where did you learn how to eat them?"

"You don't want to know."

"No, I probably don't. . . . Well, what was her name?"

"Uh, Teresa Castro. She was . . . eh, she had this . . . eh, her daddy was—"

"I don't want to know," Pepper insisted.

"I forgot all about her."

"So I can tell! Anyway, I'm sorry Mrs. Martin wasn't home. She certainly has a lovely place for being stuck way out of town. Did you see all those etched mirrors over the mantel in the parlor?"

"L. J. said they shipped everything out from New York. I guess the missus gets homesick."

"How did you know L. J. anyway?"

"He came down to Tucson one time figurin' on buying up some property near where the Southern Pacific tracks were being built. But the Apaches were runnin' wild, so he hired me to, well, sort of make sure he didn't get scalped."

"But he didn't buy a ranch down there? Did the Indians scare him off?"

"That and the fact that the S. P. owns every other section down in that country. It's their bonus for putting in the railroad. Not only that, but some of it was tied up in Spanish land grant litigation."

"So he came north?"

"He bought this place, built the house, and moved his wife and kids here. Then that summer Custer and the Seventh Cavalry got killed at the Little Big Horn. The wife's never gotten used to living out here, I reckon."

"I'd still like to meet her someday."

"Maybe you will. L. J. offered me to rep for him."

"What does that mean?"

"It means I make sure no one's stealing his beef and rebrandin' them. And I ride with the association roundup seeing that L. J. gets all his bovines sorted out. His place runs clean up to Pine Bluffs, and you know how many cattle the U. P. runs out of there."

"Where would we live?"

"That's the rub. He'd pay me year 'round, but I'd only work April through November. So he figured we would still live in Cheyenne, and I could have every forth week off during the summer to come see you."

"What did you tell him?"

"I told him it was a job for a single man. I wasn't interested."

"Really? That's what you said?"

"Yep."

Pepper scooted closer to Tap and slipped her arm through his. Then she glanced at the western horizon. "Do you think we'll make it back home before dark?"

"Nope."

Guided by the incandescent lights of the city, they rolled up Crow Creek and into Cheyenne about nine o'clock. Tap pulled up to their cottage on 17th and began to help Pepper unpack the supplies.

"Looks like we got in a big hurry to go on that picnic yesterday." He motioned to the door that stood a foot open.

"It's been open for a whole day!" Pepper groaned. "Some dog could have wandered in."

"Not to mention a footpad or a sneakthief. If you want to wait, I'll tote this gear in and light a lantern and see if everything is all right."

Pepper scampered ahead of him. At the sound of her cry, Tap dropped the food crate and raced into the house with .44 drawn.

"Look at this mess! The dogs got in here and scattered stuff all over the place!"

Tap squatted down and examined the books, papers, clothes, food, and dishes tossed on the floor of the combination front room and kitchen.

"Something . . . or *someone*? This wasn't an animal looking for food. Look in the kitchen. Somebody emptied out every shelf, closet, cupboard, and box looking for something."

"Were they looking for money?"

"Not if they were smart. With all those cattlemen's fancy homes further up 17th, there's no reason to bust into our little place."

"Oh . . . Tap," she sobbed, "it's all torn up. I had it so neat. I had it really neat, didn't I?"

"You sure did, darlin'. Come on. Don't worry—I'll help you, and we'll straighten it up. I had you, my guns, and a plate of biscuits with me. There wasn't anything left of value in here except maybe that old grand piano. What's the bedroom look like?"

Pepper scurried to the bedroom and then poked her head back out. "It's just tossed around some, but I don't think anything is missing. That jewelry I got from Miss Cedar was poured out on the dresser, but nothing seems to be gone."

A knock at the front door startled them.

"I know who did it!" a voice crackled through the night.

With gun in hand, Tap approached the doorway. A short, shriveled woman with a black shawl over her head and shoulders stood on the porch. She carried a candle.

"Who are you?"

"Mrs. Wallace."

"Our neighbor?"

"Yes."

"Eh . . . pleased to meet you, Mrs. Wallace. This is my wife."

"Pepper. Yes. I know all about you two."

"Did you say you know who did this?"

"Yes."

"Well, who did it?"

"Two bummers."

"Are you sure?"

"Yes."

"Do you know their names?"

"No."

"Have you seen them in town before?"

"No. I don't go out much."

"Could you recognize them if you saw them again?"

"No. It was late last night and even darker than it is now."

"Well . . . thanks, Mrs. Wallace. I wish I knew who they were."

"That won't be hard." The old lady hobbled down the steps and shuffled toward the street.

"Why's that?" Pepper called to her.

"Just ask the man who drove them here in a wagon and turned them loose. He drove back an hour later and picked them up."

"Someone brought them to our house?" Pepper gasped.

"Yes."

Tap followed the woman out into the street. "Do you know who it was?"

"Yes."

"Well, who was it?" he almost shouted. "Who was driving the wagon?"

She limped a little but didn't carry a cane. He could hear her shoes shuffle across the hard-packed street.

"It was Deputy Merced!"

7

"Are you sure it was Merced?" Tap pressed

"I wrote it right down in my diary." She tugged a sagging black knit shawl back up on her shoulders. "It's there all right. Every time I see something out my window—like that long kiss you gave the missus two days ago after breakfast—it's all recorded in my diary."

Tap grabbed his rifle, shoved it back underneath the carriage seat, and swung up into the rig. The black leather seat was already cold and stiff.

"Where are you going?" Pepper called.

"I'm goin' to visit Simp Merced."

"Tap, don't go tonight. You're mad."

"I got good rights to be mad."

"I'm afraid you'll go off and do something you'll regret!"

He tugged down the front of his black felt hat and glared. "I promise you, I won't regret it!"

"How about me, Tap? Will I regret it?"

"Pepper . . . I just can't allow this to happen! You don't understand. I can't let anyone think they can barge into my home and do this."

"*Our* home."

"What?"

"It's our home," she insisted. "It belongs to both of us." With lantern still in hand, Pepper sat down on the front step. "Tap, I don't feel good."

"Look, you aren't . . ." He held back the rest of his sentence. He stared ahead into the darkness of the night. Mrs. Wallace had padded her way back to her house. The street was quiet, but he could hear a general roar from the saloons on 15th and 16th Streets. He glanced back at Pepper, her knees to her chest and her arms wrapped around them.

Tap swung down out of the carriage and retrieved his rifle. "You look cold."

"I've got a chill," she acknowledged.

"Your forehead's sweating."

"Yeah. Maybe . . . maybe I got a touch of flu riding in that open carriage."

"Come on, let's straighten up some of this mess and get you to bed." He helped her to her feet.

"Thanks, honey." She faintly smiled.

"For helpin' you up?"

"For staying home tonight. I really need you to be with me."

"I don't exactly like admitting it." He sighed. "But I suppose it isn't too good of an idea goin' after Merced when I'm this aggravated."

Tap leaned down and gave Pepper a kiss on the cheek.

"Not out here," she lectured. "We don't want to give Mrs. Wallace anything to write in her diary."

It took little more than an hour for Tap and Pepper to get the house straightened up. He sat on the edge of the bed tugging off his boots while she combed her hair in front of the mirror.

"How you feelin' now, darlin'?"

"A lot better. I think it was the shock of having everything tossed around like that."

Tap yanked off his socks and rubbed his toes. "The strange thing is that I can't spot anything missing—and nothing really broken. They were just lookin' for something."

"What do you have that Simp or even those bummers want?"

Tap slapped the bed, then jumped to his feet. "The badge!" he shouted.

"The marshal's badge?"

"I told the mayor to send Simp after it!"

"Well, where is it?"

"Here in my vest pocket."

"You mean my house got turned completely upside down because of some tin star?"

"*Our* house," he corrected.

"You really think Simp is the type to hire a couple footpads to scour our house to find that badge just so he wouldn't have to confront you?"

"Yep."

"Well, if that's what the city council wants, what else can you do? Just give it to him."

"I can't do that. He'll have to come face me."

"Why? So you can provoke him to a fight?"

"You don't understand."

"I understand our house was a complete mess, and no telling what will happen next time."

Tap sat on the bed staring at the wall while Pepper climbed under the flannel sheet and heavy green comforter. She turned her back toward him and didn't say another word. Finally, he finished getting ready for bed and turned off the lantern. Pepper felt him slide in under the covers and slip his arm around her waist.

Rolling over, she stared at his face in the shadows. "What are you going to do about the badge?"

"I'm thinkin' that things like this used to be simpler to figure out before I got married."

"Are you regretting your decision?"

"Nope." He held her tight and lifted her hair off her neck and kissed her. "Do you think Mrs. Wallace can see us now?"

"Nope," she replied, with her right hand finding the back of his neck and pressing his lips to hers.

With slow, deliberate movements Tap buckled on his gun belt. Glancing back at the bedroom, he slipped the .44-40 out of its holster. He quietly spun the chambers and then replaced it. He left the canvas coat hanging on the rack and pulled on his brown leather vest. Instinctively he pulled out the badge . . . then shoved it back into the vest pocket. His hat felt cold and stiff. The braided horsehair stampede string hung down his back like an Oriental's queue. He rubbed his hand across his face and felt the stubble of a three-day beard.

I probably ought to shave. I probably ought to stay home! Lord, I don't want to do something dumb . . . but I can't let him do this to me.

The pre-dawn sunlight was reflecting off of a few scattered clouds on the eastern prairie horizon when he stepped out to the front porch and gently closed the door behind him. The cool early April morning air opened his eyes and flooded his lungs.

The street was quiet. Even Mrs. Wallace's window looked vacated. Other than a small dog's high-pitched protest, the only noise Tap could hear was the jingle of his own spurs as his boot heels struck the boardwalk.

A man without spurs is like . . . like a lady without earrings! I'll never take another job where I can't wear spurs.

At the corner of 17th and Hill Streets, Tap waited for a loaded farm wagon to pass.

"Tap?"

Rolly Hayburn was driving the rig.

"Looks like you're movin'," Tap commented.

Rolly waved his hand. "You ought to be thinkin' the same thing! Soon as those bummers down at DelGatto's heard you weren't carryin' the badge, they've been drinkin' themselves into a lynchin'."

"They're goin' to be sorely disappointed. Hager's out at the stockade at Ft. Russell. I don't surmise any of 'em are dumb enough to try that."

"I hear they got a way to get Hager back to town. And if that don't work, they're comin' after you. I reckon this town is about to blow, Tap, and I don't aim on bein' around."

"Where you headed?"

"I guess it's time for me to 'go see the elephant.'"

"The Black Hills?"

"Yep."

"What's in the wagon?"

"Cotton gloves."

"A whole wagon full of gloves?"

"The U. P. sprung a leak in a railroad car, and they got wet. Whipple and Hay wouldn't take them, so the railroad sold me the whole lot for twenty cash dollars. I dried 'em out over a fire. Figure if I sell 'em for a dime a pair, I'll turn a handsome profit. Besides, maybe I'll find me a gold mine."

"Take 'er easy, Rolly. There's some bad ones along the way still tryin' to lift your poke."

"Cain't be no worse than that rabble down at the tracks."

"You might be right about that. You haven't seen Merced, have you?"

"Nope. So long, Tapadera."

"Adios, Rolly."

Tap watched as the wagon rolled north. Then he turned and stared back toward the railroad tracks.

Where in the world did Rolly get twenty dollars? . . . But he's right about Cheyenne.

Progress.

They called trains the vehicle that would "carry us into the twentieth century." "Civilization advances on the rails into primitive lands."

We got electricity.

Fancy houses.

Paris fashions.

Fine cigars.

Irish whiskey.

Chinese silk.

And we got half the derelicts and footpads in North America who only had enough money to ride to Cheyenne. Then they cram into the roundhouse plannin' on how to get to the Black Hills— or how to steal from each other . . . or someone else.

Lord, Cheyenne's too crowded. It's easier to love your neighbor if they're scattered out some. All clustered up, they surely do bring out the worst in each other, don't they? I'd be grateful if You would take that bunch at the tracks and do some scatterin'.

Tap walked slowly north toward the courthouse and jail. He fastened the top button on his vest and blew into his hands, rubbing them together.

Lord, if Merced pushes it, I'll have to shoot him. I just can't figure it any other way.

Tap shoved the door to the marshal's office open and stepped quickly inside. Baltimore Gomez was pouring a cup of coffee.

"Tap! Where you been? We've been lookin' all over for you."

"Pepper and me got away for an overnighter out at the Martin ranch. What's happening around town?"

"You should've told someone where you was. Me and Carbine spent half the day worried that you been bushwhacked and then fretted all evenin' that you had moved out of town without sayin' goodbye."

"Well, I do have to find a job, Baltimore."

"This is peculiar around here, Tap. Me and Carbine are pullin' out too. We'll work 'til payday, that's all."

"Don't do it for me, partner. Where is that temporary acting marshal? My house got tore up, and Merced's got a lot of explainin' to do."

"No! Your house? You suppose someone thought Hager was back over there?"

"Where's Merced?" Tap repeated.

"He went out to the Fort to bring in Jerome Hager."

"Hager doesn't have to appear in court, does he?"

"Nope. Simp said it was a disgrace to call on the troops. He said it was a Cheyenne matter, and we'll take care of it here in town. He's plannin' on keepin' Hager in the jail."

"He can't do that! They'll lynch Hager for sure!"

"I reckon Simp knows that too."

"Did the judge approve of the transfer of the prisoner?"

"Judge Blair took the train to Evanston. He's holding court

over there for a couple of days. Simp said the acting marshal has the authority to transfer the prisoner."

"You and Carbine figurin' on holdin' off that lynch mob? It's a cinch you won't get any help from Merced."

"We can take care of ourselves, Tap. We don't aim to gather lead from no drunks."

Tap paced the room. "Yeah, neither did Pappy. This whole thing is crazy! You say he's bringin' in Hager by himself?"

"That's what he claimed. He said if you could do it, so could he. You reckon he'll shoot Hager on the way in?"

"No, but I figure he won't put up any resistance if a gang just happened to be hidin' in a draw or gully."

"Don't suppose there's much we can do about it." Baltimore shrugged.

"I gave Hager my word I'd see that he had a trial. There's got to be some way a man can keep his word."

"What do you aim to do?"

"Think I'll ride out to the Fort."

"What will you do when you get there?"

"I don't know. . . . Baltimore, promise me something— don't get yourself stuck in here guardin' Hager all night. Drunken lynch mobs aren't very discernin'."

"I don't aim to be here. But if I am, I could no more let 'em have a prisoner than you or Pappy could. You know that."

"Yeah." Tap sighed as he turned to leave. "I know it."

Tap carried his rifle across his lap as he rode Brownie to Ft. Russell. What few clouds were left in the air were high and thin. The leaves on the trees lining the lane to the officers' quarters looked ready to burst out and celebrate spring.

It's a git-up-'n'-go day. Time to drift on down the trail until I find something new. I'm always sorta restless when the seasons change. It's a good thing spring follows winter.

Simp Merced's blue roan was tied out in front of the commanding officer's quarters. Tap dismounted and slowly walked across the wooden front porch of the office, trying to keep his spurs from jingling too loudly. Several voices shouted inside. Tap scooted back to the corner of the building next to Brownie.

The front door swung open. A red-faced Simp Merced backed out of the office, accompanied by Col. Hollings and two other officers.

Hands flying, Merced shouted, "You're insulting the entire city of Cheyenne!"

"And if you think I'll allow just anybody to ride in here and remove a prisoner that has been assigned to our care by a United States territorial court, you're dead wrong!"

"You can't do this! I demand you release that prisoner!" Merced hollered.

"You bring me papers signed by Judge Blair or Acting Marshal Andrews and I'll—"

"I'm the new acting marshal!" Simp screamed.

"That why you're sporting that deputy's badge?"

"Look, the badge is, eh," Simp stammered, "it's . . ."

"It's over here in my vest pocket!" Tap called out. All four men spun around.

Simp's hand went for his revolver, but as soon as he saw Tap's hand resting on his Colt, he backed off.

"Mr. Andrews!" Col. Hollings tipped his hat. "Nice to see you again, and how is Mrs. Andrews?"

"Fine, thanks. She sends her greetings to all the officers and gentlemen at the Fort."

"My, can that woman dance!"

Merced stared at the colonel and then at Tap. "Andrews, I've been lookin' for you! I want my badge."

"You haven't been lookin' for me, Simp. Oh, you brought some bummers over to ransack my house, but that's because you knew I was out of town."

"Mr. Andrews, what's going on here?" Col. Hollings pressed. "Who's in charge of law and order in Cheyenne?"

Tap took a couple of steps closer. Simp backed away, then held his ground. "Well, the city council decided to fire me. Guess I wasn't enough politician for the job. But I don't figure anyone is in charge of law and order."

"I'm the acting marshal, and you know it!" Simp shouted. "I demand that you surrender my badge!"

"Come and take it yourself." Tap spoke in a low, soft voice.

"You can't bully me!" Simp growled.

Tap shook his head. "A half-grown duck could bully you!"

Simp yanked at his revolver, but Tap's had been pulled, cocked, and pointed at his head before Merced's cleared his holster.

"Gentlemen!" Hollings barked.

"Colonel, there won't be any shooting at the Fort, but I don't intend to stand here and let any man pull a gun on me, whether he's actin' marshal or not." Tap released the hammer and shoved his revolver back into the holster.

"You mean to tell me Mr. Merced really is the acting marshal?"

"It's an act, all right, but that was the decision of the city council."

"Now are you goin' to let me have Hager?" The bravado returned to Merced's voice.

The commander of Ft. Russell threw up his hands in disgust. "I allowed you to bring him out here in the first place as a personal favor to Judge Blair and the memory of Marshal Divide. I can see that it was a mistake for us to get involved in civilian criminal matters. Yes, we'll release him to your custody, but I will not, and I repeat, I will not send troops to town to gather him up at a future date. This is absurd! Do you understand that, Mr. Merced?"

"Yes, sir. That's all I'm askin' for."

"Lt. Morris, draw up the necessary papers for the transfer of the prisoner." Then turning to Tap, he cocked his head. "Just where do you fit into all of this now, Mr. Andrews?"

"I gave my word to Hager that I'd see he stood trial. Think I'll just ride along with Merced and see that the prisoner is safely brought back to the jail."

"I don't need any help!" Merced protested.

"That all depends upon what you aim to do. If you want to get Hager into jail, you certainly need some help."

"I don't need to draw a big crowd like some. I'll slip him into the city quietly."

"Seems to me a man of Mr. Andrews's proven ability would be extremely useful in sequestering a lynch mob," Col. Hollings suggested.

"He's goin' to try to shoot me in the back—that's what he aims to do," Merced whined. "He'll do anything to get appointed acting marshal."

"The only one who will be shot in the back is Hager. That's why I aim to ride along." Tap took one stride toward Merced, who again backed up a couple paces.

"Gentlemen!" Col. Hollings interrupted. "It is obvious that an impasse has been reached. Lieutenant, draw up a van and escort. We will deliver Hager back to the courthouse where we picked him up. After that it will be up to the marshal, or acting marshal, to guarantee the prisoner's safety until the trial date."

"I don't need a military escort!"

"Well, you've got one, mister! Now you wait out here by your horse until they're ready to pull out."

Then the colonel turned to Tap. "How about you, Mr. Andrews? What do you intend to do now?"

"Reckon I'll mosey back to town. Sorry for this mess-up."

"Give my personal regards to Mrs. Andrews." The colonel tipped his hat and reentered his office.

Both Tap and Simp Merced watched the officers walk back inside. "Andrews, I'm tellin' you, I'm comin' after that badge!"

"Anytime, anyplace, Merced. Let's do it right here. Come on, you're packin' a pistol, and so am I! I got the badge. Come get it."

"You ain't goin' to sucker me into a gunfight!"

"Oh, when you said you were comin' after me, you meant in the dark of night tryin' to shoot me in the back. I've seen a few pitiful lawmen in my day, but you might be the worst." Tap purposely turned his back toward Merced and walked over to Brownie. He didn't bother looking back.

That wasn't too good, was it, Lord. I don't have the temperament to be a good lawman. Too much gun smoke already in the air. A past with too many shots fired in anger, too many clowns holding .45s and fools with carbines tucked against their shoulders, too much stubborn pride. Ed Masterson . . . Old Bill

Crowder . . . Pappy Divide—they had a lawman's personality.
They could handle it. They didn't let it goad them.

'Course, they're all dead now.

Law . . . order . . . justice . . . fairness. It looks like no one in
Cheyenne wants 'em bad enough. There's probably a mighty good
reason this territory hasn't qualified for statehood.

But it isn't my fight, Lord. I just want to gather up that Pepper
girl and ride away from it all. For the life of me, I can't imagine
why it is I'm stayin'. It's got to be somethin' more than a gunfight
promise to a killer who I hope is goin' to hang for his crime.

Between Ft. Russell and Cheyenne there's only one draw deep
enough to pull off an ambush. When Tap hit the Cold Springs
Trail, he turned Brownie to the south where the little arroyo
resembled a miniature canyon. With his rifle across his lap, he
rounded the first bluff and came upon two shabbily dressed men
sitting on swayback horses in the dry creekbed. One held a cap-
and-ball revolver, and the other had a rusty Henry rifle in his lap.
Both weapons looked more dangerous to the ones holding them
than to the one being aimed at.

"You ain't goin' no further than this, Andrews," one of the men
announced, waving the Henry at him.

"How many you got up the arroyo, boys? It takes about two
dozen of you to screw up the courage to shoot a man in the back,
doesn't it?"

"You don't know who you're dealin' with, mister. Besides, you
ain't a deputy no more."

"That's right, boys. And do you know what that means? That
means if you even point those guns toward me, I can shoot you
down on the spot and claim self-defense."

Both men glanced nervously behind them. "We don't bluff
down, Andrews." The tone of the man's voice betrayed him. Tap
noticed both horses prancing.

"You two pretty experienced at this sort of work, are ya?"

"We been around."

"Glad to hear that. Let's see what kind of riders you are."

Tap blasted three shots into the dirt in front of their horses. Both mounts bucked wildly. In less than half a dozen jumps the men were slammed to the ground, and the gulch filled with dust and gun smoke. Tap heard the sound of wagons and riders bearing down on him. He swung down to the dirt, jabbed the rifle barrel in one man's ear and stamped his boot heel against the other man's neck. Holding his revolver in his left hand, he looked over at the incoming riders.

"Andrews, what in hades are you doin' here?" a wagon driver screamed.

Strappler. Eden. Trementen . . . and all the DelGatto crowd— except the boss.

"At the moment I'm thinkin' about puttin' a 200-grain bullet through the heads of these two seasoned gunfighters. So I would encourage you not to do anything to imperil their future."

"Hold off, boys!" one of the downed men cried.

"You ain't no deputy anymore. You got no business out here!" another yelled out.

"Neither do you," he hollered back. "But the reason I'm here is to save your lives."

"How do you figure that?" a man on a prancing spotted horse called out.

"In a few minutes a couple dozen soldiers from Ft. Russell will be ridin' over that rise bringin' Hager back to town in a military van. You boys attack that, and you'll have to face the wrath of the entire United States Army."

"An escort? Merced said he was bringin' him back himself. We don't believe you!"

"Well, why don't we wait right here and find out."

A man with a long, tattered topcoat and no shirt underneath rode forward. "We don't aim to be standin' out here in the clear."

"Why not? If it's just Hager and Merced like you say, who are you afraid of?"

"He's right," one of the men riding double concurred.

"But we're supposed to stay out of sight," another in the wagon protested.

Tap turned his pistol on the speaker. "Who told you that?"

"Eh . . . it don't matter. He's right. Boys, some of you line up on that side of the road," Strappler commanded. "Andrews, let them two loose."

"You mean it takes more than fifteen men to shoot Hager in the back?"

"You ain't leavin' this draw alive, Andrews. We got you out-numbered any way you count it."

"Take a look up the road. I'd say it's pretty even."

"It's the blue coats! Merced is with 'em!"

"Now if I were in your boots, I'd surely whip them old ponics and broken-down wagons back to town and make sure I was out of range of those soldier boys with Springfields."

The whole pack of men and wagons turned east, rumbling and galloping out of the draw. Tap swung up on Brownie, but he kept his revolver aimed at the two on the ground.

"Our ponies done ran off."

"Then I suggest you do the same!" Tap waved his pistol in their direction. They scampered to their feet and stumbled up the bank of the draw toward Cheyenne.

By the time the troops reached the bottom of the arroyo, only Tap was left. Lt. Morris rode over to him as the others continued on to town. Simp Merced refused to even look in his direction.

"What was all of that about?" The captain pointed to the dust trail back to town.

"I guess it was a welcome committee."

"What happened?"

"They didn't feel welcome. Do you mind if a civilian like myself rides along with you to town, Lieutenant? I'd sure like to see Jerome Hager safely in jail."

This time there were no crowds lining the streets for the entry of Jerome Hager. Only a few people poked their heads out of shops, stores, and offices to watch the troops roll down 19th Street.

Baltimore Gomez and Carbine Williams stood guard on the steps of the jail as Merced signed some transfer papers and led a disgruntled-looking Jerome Hager into the building. Tap waited with the soldiers. After their departure, he spurred Brownie to a trot toward home.

Pepper met him on the front porch. "What happened?"

"Nothin'. Except Hager's back here in jail."

"Why?"

"So the lynch mob can get to him easier, I guess. It was Merced's idea."

"Did you talk to Merced about our house?"

"Eh . . . not much."

"But you did talk to him?"

"Yeah, I guess you could say that."

"What did you discuss?"

"I think we left it that he was threatenin' to come after me if I didn't give him the marshal's badge."

"And what was your response?"

"'Anytime, anyplace.' If I remember the exact words."

Tap followed her to the kitchen.

"I don't think I like living in Cheyenne anymore," she said quietly. "We need to be out on the prairie where it's just you and me."

"I think you're right, babe. As soon as we settle up some things here and—"

"Settle up what? Revenge against Simp Merced? Don't take chances. You're my whole world," she pleaded.

Tap broke into a smile. "You know, darlin', we might spend our whole lives with nothin' but each other."

"Sounds good to me. How about you?"

"Well, I'd probably get hungry after a while," he teased.

She stuck out her tongue. "I'm having ham and cabbage soup. Are you going to eat dinner with me?"

"What's for dessert?"

"The usual."

"I'm stayin'."

"Where else would you go? You're unemployed, the last I recall."

They were halfway through the meal when Pepper jumped out of her chair and scurried to the front room. "I almost forgot!" she called out. "A man came by to see you this morning."

"Who was it?"

She carried a small scrap of paper back to the table. "His name is Tom Slaughter. He's from Pine Bluffs. Said you could reach him at the Rollins House."

"What did he want?"

"He didn't tell me. Do you know him?"

"I don't think so. Did he . . . you know, look like he was on the prod?"

"No, he looked like he'd been on the trail for three months."

"Was he ridin' a short Texas horse?"

"I guess so. I didn't pay much attention. Why?"

"Maybe he came up the trail. I'll check him out."

He tore off a huge hunk of sourdough bread and dipped it into the soup. Chomping into the bread, he could feel broth dripping across his chin. Tap wiped a faded red linen napkin across his face and brushed back his mustache.

Pepper pulled her elbows off the table and sat up perfectly straight, trying to keep her left hand in her lap. "Angelita came by this morning looking for you."

"Did you ever see anyone quite like her? What did she want to sell us?"

"Well, she did have an autographed picture postcard of Martha Maxwell—you know, the lady big game hunter."

"I bet she did."

"But I really think she wanted to talk to you about her father. She worries about Baltimore workin' down there."

"I don't blame her. With Merced at the reins, it's just a matter of time before it blows wide open. I'll go talk to Baltimore."

"When?"

"After dessert."

A smile cracked across his face and lit up his eyes and made her heart jump.

Lord, I really, really like being married.

Baltimore lounged on the front step of the marshal's office smoking a long, skinny, loosely rolled cigar when Tap rode up.

"It's mighty quiet around here."

The deputy looked up and the down the street. "You're right about that, Tap. Makes a man wonder what's bein' planned."

"I think it's about time for you and Carbine to call it quits. It's not worth it anymore."

"Would you quit if you was in my boots?" Baltimore asked.

"Probably not . . . but everyone knows I'm too pigheaded for my own good. Besides, you've got to think of Angelita. She's worried you won't live long enough to see her elected governor."

"If I can keep her out of jail."

"Don't take chances with double-crossers like Merced."

"Me and Carbine got it figured. Judge Blair wired that he'll be comin' in on the eastbound in the mornin'. We're goin' to see it through this one night and then find out what the judge has to say. We told Merced we'd work 'til noon tomorrow."

"That means they'll try something tonight."

"I don't think so," Baltimore drawled. "We didn't show Merced the judge's telegram. We think the lynch mob will hold back until we quit and they have smooth sailin'."

"Well, at least that would give the judge some responsibility in all this."

"That's what we was thinkin'."

"How's Jerome doin'?"

"He's cussin', yellin', and wantin' a bottle. Said if he's goin' to be lynched, he wants to be drunk so he won't feel it."

"Merced didn't volunteer to take the night shift?" Tap asked.

"Nope. That's another reason we figure he's plannin' on tomorrow night. He knows he'll be by himself."

Later in the afternoon, Tap rode Brownie south on Ferguson intending to turn toward the livery. Nagle and Whipple called to him from the street corner at 17th.

"Andrews, the city council wants to talk to you."

"I don't have anything to say. You fired me without even a discussion. I don't owe you nothin'."

"You owe us a marshal's badge."

"Where's the meetin'?"

"Mayor Breshnan's hotel—in fifteen minutes."

"I'm takin' Brownie to the I-X-L. Then I'll come by. But I won't be stayin' long."

Half an hour later Tap marched into the hotel owner's office. Four out of the five city council members and the mayor waited for him. All five hovered about the mayor's desk while Tap stayed close to the door. A large portrait of Abraham Lincoln hung on the wall behind the desk, peering over the men's shoulders. Stale smoke lingered in the room.

"I'll come right to the point, Andrews. We know we severed employment rather abruptly so—"

"That's an understatement."

"Well . . . that's exactly why we voted to pay you until the first of May. However, your lack of cooperation has—"

"Now you're threatenin' to take away my severance pay if I don't give you a little tin badge?"

"We will," Nagle puffed. "And we're prepared to press charges against you if you don't."

"What charges?"

"False appropriation of government property."

"You goin' to serve the warrant? Merced's afraid to come within three blocks of me."

"You're incorrigible, Andrews. We definitely did the right thing by letting you go," Felix Goldstein huffed.

"I'll tell you what you did." Tap could feel his face flush with anger. He had a strong desire to pull his .44 from the holster and cock the hammer.

But he didn't.

"You're about to bypass the American judicial system and insure that Jerome Hager hangs by a lynch mob. You appointed a bigoted, gutless bully as acting marshal. Within two days Hager will be danglin' from a cottonwood, and within a week any semblance of the law and order that Pappy Divide gave his life to sustain will have vanished. Every gang of bummers headed for the mines or drovers going to the roundup will descend on Cheyenne to raise Cain. The footpads and sneakthieves will move across the tracks and invade those fancy Victorian houses of yours. And the cemetery will have to hire another crew."

"You're overreacting, Andrews."

Tap stared at Mayor Breshnan. "Have you ever been in a town that lost all respect for the law?"

"Well, that won't happen. We just won't let it."

"You?" Tap whipped out his revolver and pointed the barrel of it toward the hotel owner. "Is that your main safe?"

"Yes, but—"

"Then which one of you is goin' to stop me from taking all the money in it?"

"What?" the mayor gasped.

Tap shoved his gun back into its holster. "That's the point. Not one of you could stop me. That's what it's like in a town without respect for the law. Me—I'm pullin' out. I don't want to watch Cheyenne get torn apart like that."

"We want the badge, Andrews!"

"I don't have it."

"Where is it?"

"It's not at my house, is it? Merced brought two men over to rip up the place lookin' for it. You ever had the actin' marshal hire men to destroy your house? It's a mighty discomfortin' feelin' for your wife, let me tell you."

"He did what? Can you prove that?"

"We had no idea . . ."

"I don't care whether I'm actin' marshal or not. But Simp Merced has the potential for lettin' this town get out of control, and you men will get all the credit for appointin' him. Your precious badge is layin' on Pappy Divide's headstone. The man who lifts it off that stone dishonors the best marshal this town's ever had. I have nothin' more to say to you." He walked toward the door.

"Since you are no longer under the employ of the city, I'm afraid you'll have to vacate the house we provided."

Tap spun around and glared at the men.

"Well . . . what we meant was, you'll certainly have to move by the end of the month."

Several hours later Tap came home to an empty house. He found a note from Pepper on the table saying she'd be back by four. Tap sat on the front porch step to wait for her.

I need you here, Pepper girl, right now. Not in an hour. Not in ten minutes. Now. There are some things—important things—to talk about. You can't just leave a note sayin' when you'll be back. I got to know where you are, what you're doin', who you're with.

At least I ought to know which direction you went.

Lord, it's time to shake the dust from my boots and leave. We don't fit in here. I don't fit in here anyway. Pepper, well, she's gettin' the hang of it. I guess I'm just a loner and a drifter . . . and I don't know how to be anything else. Maybe that's why a ramblin' man shouldn't get married.

Where is that girl anyway?

Tap walked out on the boardwalk and looked up and down 17th Street. He tipped his hat to Mrs. Wallace, standing at her post in the upstairs window, and returned to the porch. Soon he sighted the yellow hat, yellow hair, and crackerjack smile.

"Hi, darlin! I missed you!" he called out as he pulled off his hat.

"Well, yes, it looks like you did!" she teased. "You look like a miner on payday."

"We need to talk." He held the door open for her.

"We certainly do!"

"Where have you been?"

"I was down at the depot seeing Savannah off. She went to visit relatives back east. Remember, I told you."

"When did you tell me?"

"Right after dessert."

"Well . . . eh, how's she doin' today?"

"Laughing, crying, thanking the Lord all at the same time." Pepper sighed. Then her eyes lit up as she turned around to face him. "What do you think this is?" She held up a key tied to a black velvet ribbon.

"The key to your heart?"

"No, you already have that," she said. "Savannah wants us to keep an eye on her place while she's gone. In fact, she begged us to stay there while she was away. She said she'd rather have someone live there than leave it vacant."

"How long is she going to be gone?"

"A month or so. Would you consider living in the hotel? I just don't feel all that safe since the sneakthieves broke into our house."

"Maybe we should."

"Really? I can't believe it. I told Savannah there was no way you would want to stay at the Inter Ocean. You told me that you never wanted to stay in a hotel room again."

"That was before the council informed me they were kicking us out of our house."

"When?" Pepper gasped.

"By the end of the month."

"Well, I guess that definitely means we're moving."

"Yeah. Is that all right with you, darlin'?"

"This cottage is too small anyway."

"I can't guarantee anything any better in Pine Bluffs."

"Pine Bluffs?" Pepper grabbed his arm. "Did you talk to that man Tom Slaughter?"

"Yep. For about two hours."

"Did he offer you a job?"

"Yep."

"What kind of a job?"

"Brand inspector."

"Did you take it?"

"Yep."

"Will you have to be gone weeks at a time?"

"Nope."

"Don't you 'yep' and 'nope' me, Tapadera Andrews! I demand that you tell me everything!"

"Not here. Let's do it over supper at the Inter Ocean."

"Really? Can we . . . afford it?"

"Yep."

"Are we actually going to stay in Savannah's suite?"

"Yep."

She slipped her arms around his waist and held him tight. "Did anyone ever tell you that what you lack in vocabulary you make up for in good looks?"

"Yep," he replied with a wink, then jumped back to soften the blow of her fist punching him in the stomach.

Later that night Tap lay on top of the satin sheets of the bed in Suite G and listened to Pepper's rhythmic breathing. A dream had startled him awake.

He forgot what the dream was, but the room felt oppressive, foreboding. He grabbed his revolver off the floor and fumbled to light a lantern. He swung out of bed and wandered out to the parlor, half expecting someone to be waiting in the shadows. When he returned, Pepper was propped up on one elbow.

"What's the matter?"

"Something strange is goin' on."

"Did you hear something?"

"No . . . but I felt it."

"Felt it? Come on back to bed. You were havin' a bad dream."

"No, it's more than that."

"What is it?"

"Something's twisted, knotted up in my stomach—in my spirit."

"Are you sure?"

"It's evil. It feels mighty evil."

"I don't feel anything. What is it?"

"I don't know. . . . Something bad happened—something demonic!"

"But how can you—"

"Hager! Oh, Lord—that's it. They've lynched Jerome Hager!" Tap groaned as he pulled on his trousers and reached for his boots.

8

The six-foot walnut grandfather's clock in the hall between the tiny kitchen and the parlor of Savannah's suite had just begun its midnight chime when Tap left the room, tugging on his coat and checking the chambers of his Colt. He was surprised to discover that the night clerk had abandoned his post.

The streets were lit with the flicker of Thomas Edison's amazing bulbs, but not one person could be seen anywhere. The normal din and roar from the saloons along the tracks was absent, and the air hung heavy.

Lord, it's like the sulfur in the air before a fox-fire summer lightnin' storm out on the plains. I don't know why You woke me up to tell me about this. I can't do anything about it now . . . can I?

Turning east on 15th Street, he saw a mass of men near the depot. There were no street lights along the railroad tracks, and in the obscurity of night every man's clothing looked murky, every face shadowy, every expression hostile.

Everyone quiet, melancholy, ashamed. Where is he, Lord? Where did they hang him?

Tap estimated there were over three hundred men gathered in the street. In the shadows he saw the silhouette of a man dangling from a rope that had been draped from the cross arm of a telegraph pole. The men silently parted and gave him a six-foot aisle as he walked—like Moses through the Red Sea—approaching the swaying corpse of Jerome Hager.

No one said a word.

Some shuffled their feet when he walked by.

Most looked at the ground.

At a night lynchin' every face looks the same—guilty.

Tap stared up at Hager. The taut hemp rope was tied off to a broken white picket fence. The killer was hanging four feet from the ground. His hands were tied behind his back; his dirty ducking trousers covered his trail-bowed legs and the tops of his boots. His cotton shirt was ripped on the right sleeve, and one suspender was broken. Hager's bearded chin was on his chest, cocked sideways. One frightened eye was open, as if to make one last recording of those in the crowd. Tap could smell alcohol still reeking from Hager's clothes.

May God have mercy on your soul, Jerome. Looks like you got to go meet your Maker drunk. You probably got what you deserved, but it's not the way Pappy would have wanted it. They wouldn't let me keep my promise, Jerome. There's not many promises I've ever had to break, and I hate breaking this one. But it's surely too late to apologize.

Tap pulled his Barlow knife out of his pocket and began to cut Hager down.

"Hey, don't ruin my good rope!" a voice crackled in the night.

Tap continued to saw through the rope. Hager's lifeless body dropped to the ground like a sack of onions. His silent face slammed into the hard-packed earth. Tap pulled the noose off his neck. Tossing it aside, he made sure both Jerome's eyes were closed.

When he looked up at the crowd, all eyes were focused on him. "Well, you brave men, you proved that if you have a hundred-to-one odds, you can sneak out into the night and lynch a man and just bypass our judicial system. You don't need marshals or judges in this town—because you can do it for them." Tap's strong, deep voice boomed across the dark Cheyenne night like a preacher addressing those at the anxious bench. "Of course, from time to time the man will be innocent . . . but that won't bother you none, will it? At least not until it's you that's danglin' from the rope."

Tap looked down at Hager, then back at the crowd.

"Where's that actin' marshal of yours? This is his job."

Most of the men quickly deserted the mob to head back to the 15th Street saloons.

"I said, where's Merced?" Tap shouted. His voice echoed down the street to the background of retreating boot heels.

"He took off," one voice mumbled.

"Where did he go?"

"I don't know."

"When did he leave?"

"Right after Hager kilt that deputy, I reckon."

Tap froze. He felt as if a river rock was stuck in his throat. "What deputy?" he choked.

"The heavy one . . . Gomez."

Lord, no! No!

"Hager shot Baltimore?"

"Yep. In the back! Like I said, hangin' was too good for him."

"What happened to Baltimore? Did you just leave him there?"

"Last I seen, that other deputy was totin' him to the hospital. But DelGatto said he was dead."

The spokesman was now the only one left in the vacated street. Tap grabbed the bearded man by the shirt collar and almost lifted him off the ground.

"Mister, you go and get an undertaker to fetch Hager's body. And if I find out you left him lying down here, you'll be the one danglin' from a rope. Have you got that clear?"

"Yes, sir. Yes, sir." The man nodded wildly.

Running up Ferguson Street, Tap could hear only the sound of his boots hitting the stones in the street and his gasping for breath. The night boy at the livery had barely opened his eyes when Tap threw a headstall on Brownie and grabbed a handful of mane hair to pull himself to the gelding's back.

"Open the gate, kid. There's no time for a saddle!"

Thundering up the street, Tap stopped at the marshal's office. He dropped the reins to the ground and took the stairs two at a time. With the .44 in his right hand, he crashed into the abandoned office.

In the flickering lantern light, he discovered a puddle of blood in the doorway between the office and the jail cells. The door of cell #1 stood open. An amber whiskey bottle was discarded under the crude bunk, and next to it lay a small, snub-nosed handgun. Tap retrieved the gun and tromped back into the darkness of a starlit, moonless Wyoming night.

A sneak gun? A Colt cloverleaf house pistol. They said Hager shot Baltimore. Where did he get a gun? Does this belong to Hager or someone in the lynch mob?

He shoved the short-barreled rimfire pistol into his pocket and climbed up on Brownie's back.

"I know it don't feel right without a saddle, boy, but we'll both just have to suffer it through. Come on, gi-hup. Let's go!"

Kicking the horse in the ribs, Tap galloped north toward the hospital on 23rd Street, several blocks past the north edge of town.

Tap tied Brownie to a tree in front and bolted up the stairs. A man reached out of the shadows and grabbed his left arm. As he went for his revolver, a familiar voice broke through the night. "Tap, it's me—Williams!"

"Did they kill him, Carbine?"

"Not yet. Dad gum it, I'm glad you're here! Did Angelita finally find you?"

"Oh, no. I was . . . I mean, Pepper and me are staying at Savannah's. She went east. . . . How's Baltimore?"

"Doctors are tryin' to remove the bullet. Hit him dead center in the back, I guess. He was unconscious when I brought him in, but the doctor said there's no tellin' what that means if he pulls through."

"If?"

"Chances aren't too good, the doctor said."

"Where's Angelita?"

"She cried around here for a while and then ran off lookin' for you. She seems to think you can do something about all this. That girl figures you can walk on water, you know."

"I saw this comin', and I couldn't do a thing to stop it. I tried to get Baltimore to quit this afternoon. One more day! One more lousy day! Someone must have told 'em about the judge coming back."

"The whole thing's screwy."

"Can we talk to Baltimore?"

"Don't know if he's come to. I thought he was dead, Tap. I knew I couldn't stop the mob. But I figured maybe I could help Baltimore. Nothin' we can do except wait for them docs to get through with him. You want a quirley?"

Tap shook his head and then plopped down on the steps. Carbine sat down beside him and dug at his fixings.

"How did it happen, Carbine?"

"Well, me and Baltimore was figurin' on stayin' on until Judge Blair made it back. He told you that, right?"

"Yeah."

"Well, things was so quiet tonight. We kept thinkin' maybe somethin' was being planned. We decided to partner up and wait the night out together. About 9:00 P.M. we were both gettin' pretty bored when someone came to the office reportin' that there was a drunk shootin' up DelGatto's Saloon on the south side. We flipped for it. I lost. So I went to check it out and bring us some supper."

"You mean, Baltimore wanted to stay?"

"We was still plannin' on havin' a quiet night."

"When I got to DelGatto's, some bummer had barricaded himself into one of the girls' cribs, threatenin' to cut her up if anyone came through the door. You could hear her in there screamin' and cryin'. They told me the bouncer had already been shot and had to be packed out to the doc with a leg wound. So I goes upstairs to try and talk the guy out when some boys down in the bar begin takin' shots at me. Then the guy in the crib starts openin' up with a scatter gun, and I'm sayin' my prayers."

"An ambush? Someone wanted you out of the jail."

"I surmise they wanted me dead. Well, when my back was against it, a door across the hall swings open, and instead of being shot, one of the girls beckons me in. At the moment I was bein' serenaded by lead and buckshot, so I figure it's worth the chance. I dove through the door.

"She's pointin' toward a window and tells me to jump out. I oblige her and dove out the open window. I hit bad on my right knee and shoulder and sort of rolled to some cover. All the while I hear her screamin' and yellin' that I jumped out the window. She put on quite a show. Well, I limped over to a little shack by the track waitin' for them to come after me, but they boiled out of that dive and hustled up the street toward downtown."

"They were joinin' in the hangin', no doubt."

"Well, I stay there and get my breath back. Then the same thing dawns on me. Someone wanted me out of the office. So I sneak back to my mount and ride back to 18th Street. By the time I got there, they had Hager drug out of the jail and were carryin' him down the street. Tryin' to turn 'em was worse than a stampede, Tap. And when someone hollered that Baltimore was kilt, I gave up on the mob and ran into the office. Baltimore was all crumpled up near the door, bleeding bad and unconscious."

"You didn't get to talk to him at all?"

"Not a word. He really looked dead. There was a big pool of blood, and I couldn't find a pulse. I flagged down the first rig that came up Ferguson and got him here. Angelita came runnin' up about fifteen minutes later. I don't have any idee at all how she knew about Baltimore. She was bawlin' and wanted to see her papa, but they kept her back. So she went to get you, sayin' you'd fix the one who done this. She didn't find you?"

"No . . . I woke up, and the air crackled like a hangin'."

"What?"

"It's hard to explain. They were all done when I got there. I cut Hager down, but that's all there was left to do. How's your leg and shoulder now?"

"I'll be limpin' awhile, that's for sure. But with Baltimore in there packin' lead like a grizzly, I can't complain." Carbine stared out into the night and took a deep drag on the quirley. "If he was goin' to get lynched, we might as well have let them do it four days ago," he mumbled.

"That's been eatin' at me all the way out to the hospital. You try to do things proper and lawful . . . and it ends up worse. It just don't figure. Did that gun under the bunk belong to Hager? How

in the world did Jerome get a rimfire sneak gun? Or for that matter, how did he get some snake-head whiskey?"

"Hager had been drinkin'?"

"Smelt like a brewery. You know how wild Jerome gets when
he's drunk. No one came to see him, did they?"

"Nope. I told you, the whole town's been avoidin' the jail like
the smallpox."

"So Baltimore's in the office, Hager's in cell #1, and the rest of
the jail's empty. . . . Hager gets a bottle and gun, gets drunk, somehow talks Baltimore into opening the door, shoots him in the
back, runs out to the steps, and a lynch mob happens to be
standin' there."

"That ain't right, Tap. It don't add up."

Carbine crushed his smoke on the limestone steps and glanced
over at Tap. "Maybe one of those bummers broke in and shot
Baltimore."

"That could be. . . ." Tap pondered. "But some of 'em told me
they caught Hager on the steps tryin' to escape. You and I both
know Baltimore would never unlock the doors even if Hager had
a gun."

Both men sat and stared out into the quiet night. It was Carbine
who broke the long siege of silence. "Stars don't care, do they?"

Tap suddenly felt the chill of the night air as he looked up at
the blanket of stars. "What?"

"Men are born . . . live . . . die   and those stars hang right
up there in the same place. They don't care."

"Nope. I reckon they don't, Carbine. But the Almighty cares."

"That's the way I figure it too." Williams nodded. "I'm surely
askin' Him to look after Baltimore."

Tap stood up and stretched his legs. "It still doesn't add up.
There's no way Hager could get a gun . . . and there's no way
Baltimore would open the door to anyone."

"Except me. And you. And Angelita."

"And Simp Merced!"

"Simp's pretty much worthless," Carbine mused, "but he
wouldn't be a part of shootin' Baltimore, would he?"

"I reckon that's the first thing I'll ask him when I track him down. Have you seen him?"

"Ain't seen him all night."

"Seems mighty suspicious for an actin' marshal to abandon his prisoner. Do you know anyone who carries a snub-nosed Colt cloverleaf?"

"You don't see many of those around unless you're in a card room fight."

"Mr. Williams?" The voice behind them was deep, quiet, authoritative. Both Carbine and Tap jumped to their feet.

"What's the verdict, Doc?" Tap quizzed.

"Oh, Mr. Andrews! Yes, well, we removed two bullets from Mr. Gomez's back."

"Two bullets?"

"Yes. The smaller-caliber one hit the shoulder and was of minimum threat, but the other larger one hit the spinal cord."

"Is he goin' to pull through?" Carbine pressed.

"We aren't sure if he will survive the night, and if he does, we aren't sure he will be able to move anything below the neck."

"Can we talk to him?" Tap asked.

"I'm afraid not. We aren't even sure he will come to. It's a critical situation. Sorry I can't give you any better news."

"At least you didn't tell us he was dead."

"Not yet anyway."

Tap stepped closer to the doctor where the light was a little better. "Doc, eh, can I see those bullets?" Holding the two in his hand, Tap glanced over at Carbine. "The smaller one looks like maybe a .41 or .38. Look at this."

Carbine held it up to the lantern. "Looks like a low-powdered sneak gun."

"This big one is a .44 or .45, but it got mashed pretty good. Can I take these with me?" Tap asked.

"You can do anything you want with them."

"Thanks, Doc."

The doctor scooted back inside the hospital.

"What do we do now, Tap?"

"I'll try to find Merced."

"You want me to come with you?"

"You'd better sit this out and rest up that leg of yours. Besides, it doesn't seem right for Baltimore to be all alone when he's this close to dyin'. If I can find Angelita, I'll send her up to wait with you."

"You goin' to gun Merced down?"

"I'll give him whatever he has comin'."

"Cheyenne is fallin' apart. Never knowed Pappy was holdin' the whole thing together. How long do you think it will take until everyone discovers there are no lawmen left in this town?"

"I figure it won't bust loose until tomorrow evenin'."

Carbine nodded. "Sounds about right."

"I'll check with ya in the mornin'," Tap added. "And send me word if Baltimore gets worse. Remember, we're at Savannah's place at the Inter Ocean. Take care of yourself. It looks like someone's out to eliminate all the deputies."

Tap cautiously searched every dive, saloon, hurdy-gurdy, and hotel on both sides of the Union Pacific tracks for signs of Simp Merced. Most places emptied like cockroaches running from daylight when he walked through the door. It was nearly 3:00 A.M. when he gave up and went back to the Inter Ocean.

Trying to sneak into the suite without waking Pepper, he was surprised to find the lights lit in the parlor. He crept into the room, then stared across at her, wrapped in one of Savannah's thick robes, sitting on the velvet settee. Sprawled beside her was Angelita Gomez, sound asleep with her head in Pepper's lap. Pepper put her finger to her lips.

"You heard all about it?" Tap whispered.

"Yes. She showed up about twenty minutes after you left. How's Baltimore?"

"Still alive . . . but it doesn't look good. He might be paralyzed."

"Angelita's scared he's going to die. She came by looking for you."

"How'd she know we were here?"

"Mrs. Wallace told her we were at Savannah's."

"But how did—"

Pepper shrugged. "She knows everything. When you weren't here, Angelita grabbed onto me and started crying. She hasn't turned loose of me. She refused to go to the hospital because she just knew her daddy was dead. She wanted to pretend he was alive as long as she could."

"Asleep she looks like a little girl."

"She is a little girl."

"But I mean . . . the way she always acts I forget how young she is."

"You look tired too, Mr. Andrews."

"Think I'll try to sleep an hour or two. You want to leave her there and come to bed?"

"I might as well sit here, Tap. I've been sick most of the night."

"Maybe you need to see the doctor."

"Sure, he'll tell me to drink some lemon tea and rest up for a few days. It's not worth the two dollars."

"Listen, if Angelita wakes up, tell her two bullets have been removed from her daddy and that Carbine is waiting at the hospital. She can go wait with him if she wants to. I'll take her down there. Just give me a poke. Don't tell her about the paralyzed part. He may be better in the mornin'."

At 6:30 A.M. Tap rode up to the Inter Ocean and hefted Angelita up onto Brownie's back.

"You should have woke me up as soon as you got in," she scolded.

"You were sleepin', and so was your papa. I figured you both needed the rest. Carbine said he'd send word if anything turned for the worst, and he didn't, so ever'thing must be stable."

They bounced along to Brownie's stiff gait. "Mrs. Andrews is very nice."

"She certainly is."

"What does she see in you anyway?"

He glanced back at Angelita and shook his head. "I'm not too impressive, am I?"

"You're a driftin', shiftless gunfighter. Come on, there really can't be too much future in marrying such a man."

"I guess she just didn't know better."

"And she seems quite intelligent at first glance. Perhaps you remind her of her father."

"What?"

"You are considerably older than she is, aren't you?"

"How old do you think I am?"

"Eh . . . forty?"

"Forty!"

"Yes, and I'd say Mrs. Andrews is about twenty. Am I right?"

"No, you are not right!" Tap thundered. "Forty! I can't believe you said that."

"My, you're powerful touchy this morning." Angelita kicked Brownie, and he broke into a trot.

At the hospital Carbine reported that there was no change in Baltimore. He had not yet come around. After getting Angelita settled in, Tap rode back downtown. At 8:00 A.M. he entered Found Brothers' Wyoming Armory. J. R. Grueter greeted him as he scooted between two other customers standing in front of the large glass case of lever-action repeating rifles.

"Mornin', Tap."

"Mornin', J. R. Looks like you got plenty of customers."

"They come in here and look around, but no one has any money. It's been this way all spring. What can I git ya?"

"Just some advice, J. R." Tap pulled out the two spent bullets from his vest pocket. "This one looks like it came out of a .41 sneak gun to me. What do you think?"

"I'd bet on it. A snub-nosed one at that. That's why you don't have any deformity in the lead. Hardly any bore marks. Didn't hit any bone, did it? Come over here to the scales." J. R. opened a cupboard and dug through a wooden box filled with assorted sizes of lead bullets ready to be reloaded.

"This one's a .41 regular," he reported. Tap tossed the smaller of the spent bullets on the scales. The balance beam leveled out almost exactly parallel to the table.

"There you go—130 grains in each. Someone take to shootin' at you with a sneak gun?"

"Not me . . . but that bullet came out of Baltimore's back."

"How's Baltimore doin'?"

"It isn't good, J. R., but he's still alive. I guess the next two days will tell."

"How about this one?"

"Kind of feels like a .45, don't it?"

Grueter cradled the lead in his hand and then placed it on the scales. "Yep, there you go. Say, was Baltimore shot by two different men?"

"Well, at least by two different guns. It's highly unlikely that Hager had two guns in his cell."

Tap reached into his coat pocket and pulled out the snub-nosed Colt. "Could this have been the sneak gun?"

"A snub-nosed Colt cloverleaf? I reckon it could. 'Course, there's a lot of sneak guns in this town, Tap. It could have been a National, a Williamson, a Remington, a Ballard Forehand & Wadsworth, or even a Frank Wesson."

"They all make .41s?"

J. R. nodded. "And they all make sneak guns."

"Well, this one was left lyin' in Hager's cell."

"Let me see that." Grueter turned the 5 1/4-inch gun over and over in his hand.

"I sold that gun yesterday." He handed it back to Tap.

"This gun? How do you know that?"

"I don't often have people lookin' for pistols with 1 7/16-inch barrels. Besides, look at the serial number on the frame at the bottom of the grips."

"1,234? What about it?"

"1-2-3-4," J. R. explained. "I thought about keeping it myself. It would make a nice walk-to-the-bank type of gun. But this bummer came in lookin' for a cloverleaf, and, well . . . I can't refuse a cash customer."

"Who was it?"

"Oh, I don't know his name. You know how it is, Tap. They all start lookin' the same after a while—dirty, bearded, worn-out clothes, medium height, derby that looked like it had a bite out of it. Really. It had teeth marks and everything."

"Was his name Nickles?"

"I don't have any idea. But I can tell you one thing—he was not a very good liar. Told me he was leavin' for Deadwood and needed a little protection from the murdering savages. Tap, you and I know that a man would be scalped before the enemy ever got within range of that snub-nose."

"He paid in cash?"

"Ten dollars—and didn't blink an eye. Shoot, Tap, I would've sold it for seven dollars. It ain't much fun if they don't barter. Do you know him?"

"I might. The other day he didn't have enough money to buy a bowl of soup at a chophouse. Think I'd better find out if he's still in town."

"Better find him today. I heard that the DelGatto gang of bummers is pullin' out tomorrow."

"All of them at once?"

"Some old boy's got empty rigs going to Deadwood, and they're all loadin' up and goin'. I suppose none of them want to stick around after the hangin'."

"Nobody takes empties north."

"That's what I thought."

"You haven't seen Merced, have you, J. R.?"

"I heard he got shot down on the south side in that gunfight."

"No, Carbine Williams was down there, but he managed to pull out unplugged."

"Well, then . . . I don't know about Merced. The report circulatin' at the Drovers' Cafe this mornin' was sketchy. Most expect 'em to call in troops from Ft. Russell. Say, you want to sell me back that house pistol?" Grueter asked.

"If nobody claims it. What will you give me for it?"

J. R. grinned. "Four bucks."

"Four? I thought you said it was worth at least seven to ten."

"A man's got to make a decent profit."

Tap shook his head as he left the Wyoming Armory. He trotted Brownie back to the hospital. Carbine Williams and Mayor Tom Breshnan were in a heated debate in the waiting room. Both men stopped when he walked in.

"How's Baltimore?"

Carbine sauntered over to Tap and spoke in a soft voice. "He came to, and Angelita's in there with him."

The mayor stormed out the front door and down the steps.

"That's great!" Tap offered.

Carbine shrugged. "He cain't move nothin', Tap. Cain't move his arms, feet, fingers—nothin'."

"But that will come back later on, right?"

"Doc ain't promisin' nothin'. Baltimore asked to talk to you."

"I'll wait for Angelita to come out."

"No, I think he wants you in there now."

Tap started toward the door. "Carbine, what in the world were you and the mayor arguin' about?"

"He tried to talk me into bein' actin' marshal. Tap, ain't that somethin'? They offered it to a half-breed like me."

"What did you tell him?"

"I told him they had an actin' marshal."

"Did he know where Merced is?"

"Nope."

"Men don't just disappear."

"Not unless they're dead . . . or hidin'."

Tap entered the large room filled with five empty beds and Baltimore's. Angelita sat on his bed by the window, dressed in her rabbit coat, clutching her father's limp hand. Dried tear streaks crossed her round, brown face.

A sheet was drawn up to Baltimore's chin. His freshly shaven, weathered face stared straight at the ceiling. Tap leaned close to the injured man's head.

"Baltimore, it's Tap. How you doin', partner?"

The injured man turned his head a little and blinked. "Thought

I'd just sleep in today. Can you and Angelita handle things without me?"

Tap glanced over at Angelita's dark brown eyes. "Baltimore, I figure Angelita and me can handle anything in the world that comes along . . . but neither of us can get along without you. Do you catch my drift, partner?"

A tear puddled up in Baltimore's eye and rolled across his face. "You'd think they'd keep a hospital room clean enough so the dust wouldn't get in a man's eyes," Baltimore tried to explain.

"What happened last night?"

Baltimore took several deep breaths.

"I cain't move a thing, Tap."

"I know, partner . . . I know."

"Nurse treats me like I was a baby. It ain't no way to live, Tap. A man's better off dead."

Andrews brushed back a tear with the sleeve of his shirt. "What happened last night?"

"After Carbine took off to the south side, I bolted the door and started playin' solitaire. Well, it wasn't five minutes later that I hear a rap on the door, and there's Merced, come to bring the prisoner supper."

"He brings supper at ten at night?"

"That's what I'm figurin', but he was always a little strange. You said so yourself. Anyway he's the actin' marshal, so I snag a couple of biscuits, and he heads in to see Jerome. In a few minutes Merced leaves and tells me he'll be back about daylight."

"Did you check on Hager?"

"Not for a while. I reckoned he had settled down to eatin', and I was havin' a good run of luck with the cards. It gets to be about half past eleven, and I'm startin' to fret over Carbine. About then Jerome starts hollerin' about needin' a trip out to the privy."

Baltimore eyed Angelita who was concentrating on every word.

"Anyway I'm not about to haul him out back in the dark with half the town wantin' to hang him, so I step back into the jail and holler at him to use the bucket. That's when I see him with a whiskey bottle in his hand. I can't figure it. Tap, why did Simp smuggle him a bottle?"

"He must have been in on a plan to bust him out."

"It don't figure. He could have sent us home and turned 'em loose on Hager."

"I surmise that Merced wanted it to look like an escape."

"Well, I storm over to get the bottle, and he throws it on the floor empty, so I just turn to leave. I'm thinkin' that he'll pass out and sleep the night, and that might be just as well. Then I notice that the bar's down on the back door."

"We've had that braced for months," Tap observed. "Pappy was goin' to get it bricked up."

"So Jerome is a cussin' and tellin' me he'll kill me if I don't let him out to the privy. But I ignored him and turned to put the brace back in the door. Then I heard an explosion and felt pain in my shoulder. It was like a dull knife jabbed through my backside. My knees were collapsin'. I stumbled, fell. Reckon I hit my head on that iron brace because I was out, Tap, when I hit the floor."

"The first shot hit your shoulder?"

"I didn't come around until this mornin'. Nurse said I got shot twice. Can't figure that. Why would a man shoot me again if I was already out?"

"You were by the back door when you went down?"

"Yep. Tap, you reckon Hager had a gun . . . or just the lynch mob?"

"I don't know, Baltimore. But I promise you I'll find out. There was a pool of blood by the office door. That's where Carbine found you. Some of them said they caught Hager tryin' to escape out on the stairs."

"You don't say! How'd I get over there?"

"Was that front door locked?"

"Yep. Did they bust it down?"

"No." Andrews stood up and jammed his black hat back on his head. "Baltimore, I've got to go find Merced. This is more than a mob lynchin'. Someone came real close to doin' away with both you and Carbine in the same night. Merced's up to his hips in this thing, and he'll give me good answers or take lead. I don't much care which."

"Tap, before you leave. I got to talk to you . . . alone."

Baltimore tried to look over at Angelita. She set her jaw firmly and looked at Tap. "My mama died when I was two. I am not leaving while my father tells you what to do with me if he dies. It's my life, and I want to know the truth."

Tap glanced back at Baltimore.

He tried to nod his head.

"The nurse said they just can't take care of a man in my shape. They want to send me down to a sanatorium in Denver right away. Today. They say it's my only chance of pullin' out of this. I guess they work with cripples down there. Carbine said he would take me on the train and see that I get set up."

Baltimore looked again at Angelita.

"She cain't come with me, Tap. There's no place for her to live, no money, and no one to look after her there."

"I can look after myself, and you know it," Angelita declared.

Tap put his arm on her shoulder. "She can stay with me and Pepper 'til you get on your feet."

"And if I cain't ever move again?"

"She can stay with us 'til she's governor."

"And if, you know . . ." Baltimore choked back the words. "If I don't pull through?"

"We'll raise her like our own. You got my pledge on that, partner." Tap took a deep breath and rubbed his shirt sleeve across his eyes. "Can't keep that dust out of my eyes either."

Angelita pouted. "I refuse to live with such an unrelenting tyrant as Mr. Andrews!"

"Where did she learn words like that, Tap?"

"Not from hangin' around you and me, Baltimore." Tap turned to Angelita. "Mrs. Andrews would very much enjoy your company, I'm sure."

"Well, poor dear. She is a nice lady. She probably could use some better companionship than you."

"Thanks for your vote of confidence." Tap sighed. "Baltimore, I've got to find Merced before Cheyenne blows sky high. When do they want to take you to Colorado?"

"On the three o'clock train."

"Today? You can't possibly . . ."

"They say they'll take me down to the depot in a van and load me in a Pullman. I can be in that sanatorium by this evenin'. Doctor says that's my only chance. I've got to try it, Tap."

Andrews's eyes searched the room. "Carbine will be here with you, and I'll check back later. Can't figure how they can move you across the room—let alone to the depot." He turned toward Angelita. "What about it, young lady? Can we count on your company for a while?"

"Yes, but tell Mrs. Andrews I won't be home before noon," Angelita announced. "Are we going to eat at the hotel every meal, or do you make your wife cook?"

"Are you sure you know what you're gettin' into?" Baltimore asked Tap.

"Well, it more than likely won't be boring!"

Tap left Angelita by her father's bed and walked back out to Brownie.

I should have asked Pepper first. I can't decide something like this on my own. What am I thinkin'? But what could I say, Lord? If I wouldn't have been so stubborn . . . I should have busted into that saloon and shot Hager on the spot. Then Baltimore would be eatin' breakfast at the Drovers', Angelita wouldn't have tears on her cheeks, and most folks in Cheyenne would be just as happy.

Yet I just can't ride that way anymore. I'm not a driftin' gun-slinger. But I'm not much of a deputy neither. Pepper's right. I get too mad, too quick to shoot. Somewhere down inside . . . You're tryin' to get me out of this business, aren't You?

But Angelita . . . I sure hope I know what I'm doin'.

It took Tap only a short time to explain the situation about Angelita and Baltimore to Pepper. She stared out the window of Suite G. She felt weak. Dizzy. Sick at her stomach. Scared. And disappointed.

Why did he say that? If we have to raise . . . if we get stuck . . . if Baltimore dies! Lord, that's not my plan, and You know it.

We're going to get that ranch and that big house, and I'm going to have several children, and the boys will help Tap, and then I'll teach the girls . . . You know it's what I always dreamed about. It's a good dream, Lord. It's not sinful. Why . . . but it was my dream—not Yours.

"Well, what do you say?" Tap insisted.

Why did he just tell Baltimore? He could have . . . Well, he could have said he had to check with me first. I wouldn't have agreed to it without asking him. I mean, if Angelita had asked me, I would have said yes . . . wouldn't I?

"Darlin'?" he pressed.

She took a big, deep breath and spun on her heels to face him. "Of course, we'll do it! That's what friends are for. It's just that I've never had any friends who had children. Now it will require a change of thinking, and we'll need a larger place in Pine Bluffs. You don't suppose we could afford a two-bedroom home, do you? Wouldn't that be grand? And clothes—does she have many clothes? Will we need to buy some things? I wonder what she likes to eat. Do you know?"

"Cinnamon rolls."

"What?"

Tap threw his arms around Pepper. "I'm sure you can figure out all these things. Angelita is very opinionated. She'll let you know."

"Seriously, how long do you think she'll be stayin' with us?"

"Oh, you know, if this sanatorium is any good, and if Baltimore starts regaining use of his arms and legs, well, I'm sure he'll want Angelita closer than Wyoming."

"And what if he doesn't get better? What if he doesn't pull through?"

"Well," Tap said clearing his throat, "I guess we got ourselves a half-grown daughter."

Pepper stared at Tap.

"What is it?"

"I've been thinking that maybe this is the Lord's way of providing us with a family. Perhaps that doctor in Denver was right. Maybe I really can't have children and . . ."

The tears began to roll down Pepper's cheeks. She sniffed them back and began to cough. Then she sat down on the settee and dropped her head into her hands.

"Darlin', I think you ought to go to the doctor. You've been feelin' puny for a couple weeks."

"You know perfectly well there's not one thing he can do for a cold. You told me that yourself last February when you were sick."

"I don't have to listen to my own quotes, do I?"

"You most certainly do!" She took a deep breath and stood up. "I'm all right—really. Now let me get things arranged for Angelita. Will she be home by noon?"

"Home? This is Savannah's suite. It's not even *our* home—let alone Angelita's."

"You know perfectly well what I meant, Tapadera Andrews. Now don't you have something better to do than stand around in my way? Tell Mr. Lavelle to send up a cot and some bedding. We'll put it over by the wall."

"Yes, ma'am." He jerked down the brim of his hat and strode out through the doorway.

After finishing his chores, Tap scooted out of the Inter Ocean Hotel and down the boardwalk toward the tracks.

Lord, are You sure I'm ready for this? Last year I'm tossed into prison because Rena shot her own husband. Now I'm a married man lettin' a ten-year-old huckster that I've only known for three months move in with us. My life used to be routine. Planned chaos maybe—but planned. All I had to look out for was me. Now You know I didn't do a very good job at lookin' after myself. How in the world can I take care of Pepper and Angelita?

I'm surely goin' to need Your help.

Tap trudged into Tom Breshnan's hotel office.

"Andrews! We've been wanting to talk to you."

"I'm lookin' for Merced. Where's your marshal, Mayor?"

"You mean acting marshal."

Tap stomped across the office, and the mayor retreated to the far side of his big, cluttered desk. "I've got to talk to Simp Merced. Is he still on the payroll?"

"Well, yes . . . we haven't seen him since the lynch mob grabbed Hager. I'm afraid he will have to be released for dereliction of duty. We might have acted hastily in suspending you, and we wanted to know if you were interested in—"

Andrews rubbed the back of his neck, took a deep breath, and tried to relax. "Mayor, I'm tryin' real hard not to get angry here. I've no intention of resuming work for you. But it's mainly because I figure I'm not the right guy for the job. If I were you, I'd pay good money and hire a seasoned marshal out of Dodge City or Wichita or Silver City."

"Yes, yes, but we need some leadership right now!"

"Then you better find yourself a man in a hurry. I came here to find out if Baltimore Gomez, a deputy marshal critically injured in the line of duty, would get his medical bills paid by the city."

"Oh, yes . . . well, certainly we will do what we can."

Andrews nodded and pushed his hat to the back of his head. "I figure Simp Merced knows something about why and how this happened. I intend to find out."

"We think perhaps he left town."

"Why would he do that? He obviously wanted Jerome Hager lynched."

"We don't know, but we do know that we need adequate law enforcement immediately until some permanent solution can be secured."

"Mayor, you're askin' the wrong man."

"You refuse to help us even for a few weeks?" the mayor puffed.

"I've got another job. We'll be movin' as soon as I figure out who all shot Baltimore."

The mayor paced toward Tap. "Hager shot him in the escape attempt, of course. What's there to figure?"

"Now just how do you know that?"

"Well . . . it—it said so in the *Daily Leader*."

"And did it say what happened to Simpson Merced?"

"Eh, no."

"Then I'm goin' to keep lookin'."

"But what will we do if we have another ruckus?"

"Get the governor to call for the troops at Ft. Russell."

"But—but the governor's in Washington pressing for statehood. We can't admit to being unable to police Cheyenne. What would that look like?"

"Then you better pin the badge on and do the job yourself."

The mayor mumbled something else, but Tap was out the door and into the lobby. He pushed out the tall cut-glass and oak doors and turned toward the Inter Ocean.

It was Angelita who met him at the door of Suite G. "You're late for dinner, you know!"

"How's your daddy?"

"He's sleeping a lot. I guess that's good. Do you know that Mrs. Andrews and I have had dinner ready for eleven minutes?"

Walking into the tiny cubicle that served as a kitchen in the hotel suite, Tap slipped his arm around Pepper's waist and kissed her neck.

"If you two are finished with that folderol, we can eat now," Angelita announced. "I've got business in the lobby at half past one."

"What kind of business?" Tap asked.

"Private business." Angelita lifted her nose and refused to look at Tap.

Lord, help us.

Tap had just pushed back his chair and was drinking his second cup of coffee when a blast from the other side of town rattled the windows. Angelita jumped and ran to look out.

Tap stood to his feet and began to strap on his gun.

"You're not a deputy anymore, Mr. Andrews."

"There's a building on fire," Angelita cried.

"Which one?"

"I can't tell. . . . It's over where those houses are."

"Which houses?" Pepper asked.

"You know, on 17th where you and Mr. Andrews used to live."

9

Tap watched the bright yellow flames jab the Wyoming sky as he rode east on 17th Street. A crowd of onlookers and volunteer firemen surged ahead of him on foot, horseback, and wagons. He had just passed Ransom Street when the sight ahead caused his stomach to cramp. His neck stiffened, and he reached instinctively for the rifle in his scabbard.

"No . . . no . . . not our house!" he cried out as he spurred Brownie to a gallop.

Lord, why is this happening? It's like the whole town's started to crumble and fall into the devil's hands.

The faded cedar shingles on the roof of the house now sent flame twenty-five feet into the air. All three rooms of the cottage were completely engulfed. The spectators stood in the middle of the street staring at the inferno.

"We cain't save anythin', Andrews!" one man at the pump wagon called. "We'll try to keep them other houses from catching on fire!"

For several moments Tap just sat in the saddle and stared.

Lord, we had a few things. We were just startin' out. . . Hasn't Pepper been through enough to last a lifetime? Where were You? Couldn't You have kept this from happening?

He tied Brownie off to a post in front of Mrs. Wallace's house. The heat and bluster from the fire rolled across him like a Mojave wind in southwest Arizona. He banged on his neighbor's front door. No one answered.

Turning the crystal handle of the door, he stuck his head inside. "Mrs. Wallace? Mrs. Wallace, it's me—Tap Andrews from across the street. Are you all right, Mrs. Wallace?"

All he could hear was the roar of the fire and the excited voices in the enlarging crowd. He turned back to the street. Brownie pranced at the increasing heat of the fire. The front room wall collapsed and sent sparks out into the street. He led Brownie west on 17th and glanced back to see the fire crew pumping water on the roof of Mrs. Wallace's house.

"Tap!"

It was a shrill, desperate voice coming toward him.

Spinning around, he saw Pepper and Angelita pushing their way through the mass of gawkers.

"Pepper!"

"Oh, Tap . . . oh . . . not our house, Tap."

He put his arm around her and held her close as she sobbed. Then he felt another hand clutch at his arm. Angelita had tears rolling down her cheeks. The three were still standing there when the fire began to wane and the crowd dispersed back toward downtown.

"Well . . . ladies, it won't do us any good to stand and stare. When April's burnt, there was nothin' left worth savin'. I guess the same is true with us. It's too sad to stand here and watch."

"Mrs. Wallace!" Pepper gasped.

"She's not at home. I checked. Must be at the—"

"No," Pepper interrupted. "Mrs. Wallace is at the hotel. She ran to tell us the place was on fire."

"She ran all the way downtown?"

"Yes. Poor dear—she was so worn out we had her lie on the sofa."

"She said someone blew up your house," Angelita disclosed.

"She said what?"

"She said someone tossed dynamite into the house!"

Tap swung up into the saddle. "Come on, you two. We're riding back!" He reached down to pull Pepper up.

"We'll walk back. Go ahead. My stomach . . . it's . . . Well, I'm feeling sick."

"Ever since I spotted our house on fire, I started feelin' sick myself," he admitted.

By the time Tap reached the Inter Ocean Hotel, Mrs. Wallace was on the boardwalk walking east. Her untamed shocks of gray hair were barely concealed by the black crocheted shawl.

"Mrs. Wallace," Tap called as he swung down from the saddle. "Mrs. Wallace!"

"My house—did they get my house too?"

"Eh . . . no, ma'am. The firemen soaked it down, and it will be okay."

"Well, praise the Lord!" she rejoined.

"Who did this, Mrs. Wallace?"

She stopped to shade her eyes from the sun and looked up at Tap. He could see a sparkle in her tired, weathered gray eyes. "Young man, I did praise the Lord that you and your lovely new bride weren't in the house when it exploded. In twelve years of living in Cheyenne, I've never been around anyone quite as . . . well, how should I say it? Anyone who got into trouble like you. Did you have things happen like this when you went to school? I was a schoolteacher, you know."

"What did you mean by an explosion?"

"It started when I just happened to notice a couple of men knocking on your door."

"Two men?"

"Yes, and I thought it quite peculiar that those two would want to visit you."

"Which two?"

"The same ones that tore the place up the other night."

"Was Merced with them?"

"Oh, my, no. I understand he hasn't been seen since the hanging."

"Go on—what happened after they knocked on the door?"

"Then they went to the wagon for those pails."

"Pails of what?"

"Well, I certainly didn't know what they had in the wagon, but they carried a couple pails of liquid into your house. When they came out, your front window was open, and the pails were empty. One of them yanked out a stick of dynamite and lit it with a match. Then he tossed the dynamite through the window. It was a very good toss. Well, I dove for the bed."

"They purposely blew up my house?"

"Oh, my yes. I believe they did a rather good job of it. Well, I slipped out into the back alley and ran all the way to the Inter Ocean. You know, I haven't run that much since the all-girl Fourth of July races in '45 in San Felipe de Austin."

"You were in Texas in '45?"

"I was in Texas in '36, young man."

Pepper and Angelita arrived, and Tap signaled a passing Tom Sturgis carriage. He talked the driver into giving Mrs. Wallace a lift back to her house.

"What do we do now, Tap? We don't have anything except what's at the hotel! Oh, Tap, why did we come to Cheyenne? We should have found a place in the country."

"Darlin', we'll pull it together. You pack up everything we have at the hotel. I want us to leave for Pine Bluffs before dark."

"Today?"

"More than just our house is about to explode. I don't want you two anywhere near it."

"And what about my father?" Angelita asked.

"We'll see that he and Carbine are on the train. Then I want you two started for Pine Bluffs."

"What about you? Is there goin' to be a gunfight?" Pepper asked.

"I'll take care of some unfinished business. Then I'll catch up with you before dark."

"Merced?"

"Yeah . . . and some bummers . . . and whoever is organizing it. Simp doesn't have the brains or the money to organize an afternoon tea—let alone something like this."

"Tapadera Andrews, we aren't leaving without you," Pepper insisted.

"This is not a time for debate. I need you to—"

"We aren't leaving. So just forget that and come up with another plan."

"I didn't ask you. I told you!" he huffed.

Pepper put her left hand on her hip and waved the right one at Tap. "You are telling me to do something that I am not capable of doing! So just find a different plan. If you must have it out with Merced, then give me your shotgun, and I'll ride beside you. I told you months ago that I intend to be by your side on the day you die, and I will surely die with you. You don't have any choice in the matter."

Angelita stepped in between them. "I can cluster five shots in a fence post at twenty-five feet with a pistol," she offered.

"Look," Tap stormed, "I don't even want to talk about it!"

"Good. Now where are some guns for us, and what do you want us to do?" Pepper pressed.

"You're serious, aren't you?"

"They blew up my piano."

"You play the piano?" Angelita asked.

"No," Pepper asserted, "but that's not the point. Now, Andrews, what's our next step?"

"Well," Tap announced, "Angelita, I want you to go up to the hospital and help Carbine get your father to the depot. Tell him what's happened." He waved both hands as he talked. "Darlin', I'm serious. I want you to pack up our things. We are leavin' town."

"I'll need to clean Savannah's a bit before I leave."

"You'll have time. I'll go get a wagon rented. At three o'clock, I want you to go to the terminal and pick up Angelita. Her daddy and Carbine should be on the Denver train by then."

"Where are you goin' to be?"

"I got to find out what we're up against here," he insisted.

"Tap, I'm going to be beside you when the shooting starts. Do you understand?"

"You've got to let me take care of this my way!"

"Why?"

He looked her straight in the eyes. "Because I don't know any other way to do it."

"We want guns too," Pepper repeated.

"The shotgun and extra Colt were in the house. I'll stop by Feund Brothers and pick up a couple more. We're leavin' Cheyenne. Ever'body know what they're doin'?"

"Yes, sir, Capt. Andrews," Pepper teased.

Angelita cocked her head and squinted her eyes. "Does he always say ever'body instead of everybody?"

"Only when he's in a hurry." Pepper turned and took a big, deep breath. "Someone's got to put an end to this, don't they?"

"Yep. But I'm kind of surprised that you see it too."

"Something snapped in me. This has just got to stop—right now before another lawman is shot or another house blown up."

"You surely do look handsome when filled with righteous indignation." Tap kissed her on the lips. "Be careful, darlin'."

"You too, cowboy."

"Well," Angelita pouted, "don't I get a kiss?"

Tap leaned down.

"Oh, sure—kiss me on the cheek!"

"Young lady, every kiss better be on the cheek for at least ten years."

"Ten years! Are you kidding me? I'll be an old maid by then!" Angelita suddenly skipped north on the boardwalk.

Pepper shook her head and looked back at him. "I want to be by your side, Tap Andrews. Don't you let me down."

After renting a wagon at the I-X-L, Tap drove to the Wyoming Armory. The door was locked, but a clerk carrying a trapper model '73 unlocked the door and let him in.

"Leave your weapon by the door and come in, Mr. Andrews."

"Do what?"

"Your pistol—you'll have to empty your holster."

"Since when?"

"Since about two hours ago!" a voice boomed from the far wall.

J. R. Grueter, with a linen bandage wrapped around his forehead, was sweeping up glass in front of a broken gun case.

"J. R.! What happened here?"

"A dozen bummers were in here gawkin' like always when that house blowed up. Well, the hired help hustles out to the street to see what's goin' on. I'm workin' in the back, but I step to the storeroom door, and I hear a crash. I run up front and catch 'em pullin' repeatin' rifles out as fast as they could. I lamed one and took a carbine barrel alongside the ear. They didn't have time to load 'em, or we would've had a war, I reckon."

"How many did they get?"

"Twelve '73 carbines. That's almost $250! Until we get some law back in this town, every man's got to leave his weapons at the door. Did you ever see a town fall apart so fast?"

"There's a strange feelin' out there—ever since that lynchin'," Tap agreed.

"I think you're right. That's what's so peculiar. It's like the law died with Jerome Hager. And I never knew a man who needed to hang more than him. Was that fire up by your house?"

"It *was* my house, J. R. They blew it up."

"Who was it?"

"A couple of the bummers."

"Why your house? You ain't even a deputy anymore."

"Maybe it was a diversion. It sure made it easier to lift your Winchesters."

"It's a mighty drastic way to steal rifles."

"There's something mysterious goin' on, that's for sure."

"You think I ought to pass the word among the merchants? It might just be a good day to close early and sit on our receipts."

"You could be right, J. R. You better tell the bankers too. But before you close up, I need a favor. I lost my shotgun and a pistol in that fire. You got a couple of loaners?"

"Tell you what. You take any guns in the store you need. I'll supply the bullets. When you're done, you can either bring 'em back or buy, whatever you want."

"Let me sign some paper on that."

"No need. Your word's good, ain't it?"

Tap stared at the gunsmith. "Yep."

"So's mine. Good luck, Tap."

"Thanks, J. R."

"You goin' to wear the badge again?"

"Nope."

"I've seen miners with cabin fever, womenfolk who succumb to prairie hysteria, Indians with bitter-water delirium, but I ain't never seen a whole town go crazy all at once. It's scary."

"Give me an extra box of ready-made .44-40s. My reloadin' gear went up in the blaze."

"Don't get yourself in more trouble than you can handle, Tap. Stores and houses can be rebuilt, but you only get one life."

"You're right about that, J. R." Tap stuffed some shells into his vest pocket and carried the guns to the well-guarded door.

After leaving the wagon and guns with Pepper at the hotel, he rode Brownie south toward the tracks. Alex DelGatto's saloon and dance hall was not the biggest on the south side of Cheyenne. Nor was it the fanciest.

It certainly couldn't be called the nicest.

But it was the wildest, noisiest, and most dangerous.

Open twenty-four hours a day, it was one place in town that always roared.

But today the front door and windows were boarded up.

"When did DelGatto's close?" Tap shouted to a man reclining on a bench in front of the saloon.

The man, whose slouch hat lay over his eyes, didn't move. "This mornin' at daybreak."

"Where's DelGatto?"

"Gone."

"Where?"

"Don't know."

"How about Simp Merced? Have you seen him?"

The man pulled the hat off his eyes and propped himself up on his elbow. Shading his face with his left hand, he called out, "Are you Andrews?"

"Yep."

"I was supposed to tell you that Merced went south."

"To Denver?"

"Nope. Just south of town a ways."

"Anyone with him?"

The man lay back down and pulled the hat over his eyes.

"Don't know. They didn't tell me that."

"Who's they?"

"Don't know."

The bullet from Andrews's Colt .44 ripped the wood siding only inches above the man's head, causing him to leap to his feet with a wild, startled look.

"I said, who told you to tell me Merced went south?"

"Eh . . . Nickles—he told me that. Gave me four bits just to lay here and wait for you."

"Where's Nickles?"

"I don't know nothin', mister. Honest. I told you just what was told me. Nickles has jingle in his jeans. Maybe he's out spendin' it."

Tap's pistol was drawn when he burst through the door of Raelynn Royale's Palace Dance Hall. The place was almost deserted. The bouncer got within two feet of Tap and took a blow to the side of his head from the barrel of the Colt that dropped him to the tobacco-juice-and-liquor-stained floor. Leaping the stairs three at a time, Tap kicked open a door marked "Lucky 7"—to the screams and curses of the working girls and patrons.

He had just kicked in the third door when he spotted Nickles holding his derby and crawling out the second-story window to the balcony. The room had a huge mirror on the ceiling that almost made Tap dizzy as he was confronted by a big woman with auburn hair hanging to her knees and a carving knife in her left hand.

"You get out of here mister," she growled. "You ain't comin' in here unless you paid downstairs."

"I'm goin' through that window after that man."

"You ain't goin' through my window!"

Tap's shot shattered the ceiling mirror and crushed the girl's resolve. She dropped the knife and went running past Tap and out into the hallway of cautious onlookers. He dove through the open window and hit the balcony with a somersault, ending up on his knees. The man had just shinnied down to the street, and Tap hurdled the railing and crashed into him below.

Tap came up with one hand in the man's oily hair and the other jamming his revolver into the man's ear.

"We're goin' to talk, Nickles!"

"I don't know nothin'!"

A small crowd started to line the street in front of the dance hall.

"You bought a snub-nose from Feund Brothers. Who did you sell it to?"

"I never bought no gun!"

"The same gun was found in the jail next to where a deputy was shot in the back. You willin' to stand charges for that crime? You saw what happened to old Hager. He shot a lawman in the back. You aim to be lynched too? Who'd you buy it for? I got a witness that says he sold you that exact gun."

"He'll kill me!"

The explosion from Tap's gun sent Nickles leaping into the air as the bullet struck the rocks beneath his feet. Tap never loosened the grip on the man's hair. Nickles staggered to his knees, but Tap yanked him back to his feet.

"Well, then, the only choice you got is whether to be killed now—or later. Where's Merced?"

"It weren't Merced. It was Alex DelGatto. He gave me a ten-dollar bonus for buying it for him. I wasn't up at the jail! Shoot, I got drunk and passed out and missed the hangin'. You got to believe me."

"I asked you, where's Merced?"

"Turn loose. You're rippin' my hair out!" the man screamed. "He's with the others, I reckon—waitin' to put a bullet in your head."

"And where's that?" Tap threw the man to the road and jabbed the revolver hard against his Adam's apple.

"Out near Hazard's Corner, I think. I ain't been out there! I'm not a part of that bunch," he choked.

Tap released his grip on the man and stood up, jamming his revolver back into his holster. Leaving Nickles lying in the street, Tap tramped toward Brownie.

"I hope they gut-shoot ya!" Nickles hollered.

A shot from the second-story window of the dance hall kicked dirt in front of Brownie, and the horse shied away, tugging at the tiedown. Swinging into the saddle, Tap spurred the gelding and galloped south.

Lord, it's just like all hades has busted loose in one place.

The trail to Hazard's Corner started southwest of Cheyenne and paralleled the Denver Pacific rail line. Other than that, Tap knew nothing about the road. It was a gentle, rolling grassland of mostly unfenced range. Tall mountains hovered on the distant western horizon. The still-brown prairie harbored no trees, and even the sage and the yucca were widely scattered.

Merced waits out here somewhere. Maybe DelGatto . . . maybe a dozen others armed with repeating rifles.

Maybe.

I can't believe they'd go through all of this just to try and get me out here. There's got to be more to it than that.

This whole thing is like a stampede of evil, and someone's got to ride point and turn the demonic herd. It's like a battle to decide whether good or evil will control Cheyenne. I just don't know what I'm doin' in the middle of this. You need a preacher or someone more spiritual.

Preferably one who's a crack shot.

The two cottonwood trees were still more than two miles away, but they were the only thing that broke the monotony of the rolling rangeland. Tap guessed that next to the trees would be a spring, some corrals, and maybe a cabin. Riding Brownie into a shallow coulee, he slipped out of the saddle and onto the sandy soil. Hiking up to where he could survey the horizon without providing an obvious silhouette, Tap pondered his next move.

Pepper and Angelita only needed two trips down the big mahogany staircase in the Inter Ocean to load their things into the wagon Tap had rented. Pepper left a letter on the entry table for Savannah and then gave the keys to the hotel manager. She thought about driving by her house for one last look, but she decided it would be better not to.

Carbine Williams limped toward them in front of the hospital toting a rifle.

"Mrs. Andrews. Angelita." He tipped his hat. "You two had better come in here and wait while we load Baltimore."

Pepper and Angelita left the rig and scurried into the waiting room.

"Why are we doing this, Carbine? Are you expecting trouble?"

"Already had it. A wagon drove by and twice pumped a couple of shots at me while I sat out on the porch."

Angelita hurried down the hall to her father's room. "Who was it?"

"Don't know. But I couldn't go chasin' after them and leave Baltimore. It's strange, Mrs. Andrews. It's just like they was baitin' me. Wantin' me to chase them. You know, just like the Sioux do when they lay a trap."

"Why would anyone shoot at you?"

"I think things are beyond figurin' out. But the mayor came by and gave me and Baltimore our pay."

"Do the doctors really say Baltimore can be moved?"

"I think they're worried that they can't treat him or protect him. Here comes some help to move him."

Pepper glanced up to see a large woman approaching them.

"I've seen trains smaller than that ol' gal," Carbine whispered.

The depot was crowded with anxious-faced citizens leaving town. One of the ticket agents suggested that Carbine place Baltimore's stretcher in the baggage room and that they all wait there. Angelita and her father talked in low tones.

Pepper told Carbine about the explosion and fire and filled him in on what she knew about the robbery at the Feund Brothers' Wyoming Armory. He just kept shaking his head.

"Someone is tryin' to shoot or chase off every lawman in town," he offered. "They must be planning on robbing a bank."

"Tap had Mr. Grueter alert the businesses and banks."

"The mayor said he had alerted the governor to the possibility of needing to call for the troops at Ft. Russell."

Pepper peeked out at the crowded waiting room. "Seems to be a good time to get out of town."

"I reckon they're right," Carbine pulled out his makings. "You worried about Tap?"

"Yes . . . I guess it shows, doesn't it?"

"Well, I'll tell you one thing. That man of yours seems to get better as the situation gets worse. He might get shot in the back someday like Pappy. But I don't think there's a man alive who could take him straight on. He's so stubborn he could bluff the hide off a bull buffalo. He won't have any trouble with Merced."

"I keep thinking about a dozen stolen repeating rifles pointed at him."

Tap figured it would take him two hours to sneak up on the corrals.

I'm not even sure Merced and the others will be there. Lord, if they're there, I'd rather have it out at the corrals than in town. I know I told Pepper she would be with me, but I can't wait any longer. It's time to settle up.

He scooted down the dirt embankment to his waiting horse. "Come on, Brownie. We got work to do!"

Tap spurred the horse to climb out of the coulee. Then he returned to the one-horse trail that led to the cottonwoods. He was about five hundred yards from the corrals when he began to count the horses.

Three? Where's the others? Maybe there's only three. Maybe the others are lyin' in ambush. Maybe this isn't Merced's gang at all.

Tap kept riding straight at the cottonwoods. His '73 Winchester lay across his lap. The long-range, upper-tang peep sight was flipped up. A 40-grain cartridge was in the chamber. The hammer was cocked.

He got within fifty yards of the building and then called out, "Merced, you in there?"

There was no answer.

Make your play, boys. This is as clear a shot as you'll get.

At the first puff of gun smoke, he spurred the brown horse and then leaped from the saddle, rolling behind an adobe water trough. Brownie kept running for the trees, and three shots were fired. Tap silenced the attack with one shot through the doorway that ricocheted off the back wall.

Boys, you already missed your best chance.

Tap dove to the end of the trough where there was a little protection from the east and west just as several shots flew from the cottonwoods. Movement in the corrals on the north side caught his eye.

Someone's using the horses for cover!

He raised up, and two more shots sprayed adobe near him.

Tap's first blast dropped the red roan. The second hit the gunman in the middle of the rib cage and slung him back under the prancing hooves of the other two horses.

"He shot Campbell!" a voice in the building cried out.

Four more rapid shots kept Tap pinned to the ground. His next bullet brought down the short sorrel gelding.

"You shot my horse!" someone screamed. Suddenly a man with thick beard and ragged duckings darted from the cottonwood trees, firing shot after shot from a new '73 carbine.

Andrews raised up to face the charging man and fired. The first bullet slowed the gunman. The second laid him motionless. Tap now crawled back behind the adobe water trough so that it stood between him and the doorway. Three shots slammed into the sunbaked clay horse trough. Tap rolled to the end of the trough and fired two shots that ricocheted inside the building.

He kept low, waiting for a reply.

None came.

Did I wing him? Is there really only one man in there? Merced must be the one inside. If I could sneak around, maybe I could climb down through that busted roof.

Or he could climb out that busted roof.

Tap fired two shots into the open doorway and charged just as a rider leaped the one remaining horse over the rough-cut rail corral.

"Merced!" Tap yelled.

The top rail snapped and splintered when the horse's left rear pastern slammed into it. The horse stumbled to its knees. Merced tumbled over the head of the horse and crashed into the dirt. He crawled on hands and knees to retrieve his revolver, but Tap's shot exploded the hard-packed clay dirt just a couple of feet in front of him.

"Andrews, you're crazy! You can't get away with killin' two innocent men. I'm going to have to arrest you."

"Merced, you couldn't arrest a dead cat. You three started throwin' lead before I ever got off my horse."

"That ain't the way I'll tell it in court." Merced, still on his hands and knees, yelled with his head down as if addressing the dirt.

"What makes you think you'll live through this day—let alone appear in court?"

"Because my gun's laying over there, and you don't have the heart to shoot an unarmed man."

"But you aren't an ordinary man, Merced. You're the type to lie to get a job, hire men to ransack a house, or even pay them to blow it up. Why, I do believe you're even the type to shoot a fellow deputy in the back when he's unconscious from another wound."

"I didn't shoot Baltimore!" Merced blurted out.

"Somebody did." Tap kept his cocked .44 pointed at Merced. Walking over, he jammed his boot heel in Merced's back, forcing him to the ground. "You're goin' to wish that you went for that gun."

In a matter of minutes, Andrews had Merced's hands tied tight behind him and a rope looped around his waist.

Tap mounted Brownie and dallied the free end of the rope around his saddle horn.

"What are you doin'?" Merced shouted.

"I'm goin' to ask you a couple questions. Where did the others go, and is DelGatto the one leading this outfit?"

"I ain't goin' to tell you nothin'!"

"Then get up. You're walkin' back to Cheyenne."

"I'm not goin' anywhere," Simp insisted.

"Suit yourself."

Tap spurred Brownie, and the gelding broke into a trot. When the rope drew taut, Merced flew into the air and landed on the seat of his trousers screaming. Tap dragged him that way for half a mile. When he finally stopped, Merced was covered with dirt from head to foot and was screaming and cursing. Turning around in the saddle, Tap yelled back, "I'm going to ask you once more. If I don't get an answer, we'll go twice as far. Where are the others who stole the rifles, and who's the one bankrollin' this operation?"

"You can rot in—"

Brownie was at a lope before Merced ever completed the sentence. Tap turned left and dragged Merced through the mud and weeds at the bottom of a shallow draw.

When he turned around this time, he could see that Merced's britches were ripped and one leg was starting to bleed.

"You son of . . ."

Tap slowly worked Brownie to the top of the draw and let slack into the rope. Merced tried to stand, but by then Tap had circled around. He jerked the bound man back to the ground.

"Now, Merced, between you and me is a twelve-foot patch of prickly pear cactus. I will ask you only one more time. Where are they, and who's behind it?"

"You can shoot me, but I won't say anything!"

"Of course, you won't say anything if I shoot you. That's why you're still alive. This one's for Baltimore!"

Tap stretched his feet wide of Brownie and began to slam them into the horse's side, but he held back at the last moment and kept the horse steady with taut reins.

"NO!" Merced screamed. "They're all at the depot!"

"What depot?"

"The U. P. in Cheyenne. You can't get there in time now!"

Tap yanked Merced off his feet and dragged him toward the cactus. Merced struggled to his feet and tried to run along and keep his balance, yelling and cursing as he stumbled. Being dragged headfirst, he screamed out when his arms hit the cactus thorns. "Wait! It don't matter now. . . . The whole country will know about it by tomorrow morning."

Tap rode Brownie back around the cactus patch and left the rope slack. "What's at the depot?"

"More gold and silver than you'll ever see."

"On a westbound train?"

"Yeah. Ain't that a kick? There's $500,000 in gold bars being traded for a million in Aztec silver."

"You'll never get it. They'll have troops guardin' those kinds of purses."

Pepper, Angelita, Baltimore, Carbine—they're all at the depot!

"That's the good part. Some guy in Denver is smugglin' this in on the sly, so there won't be any guards. And I end up with $100,000!"

"Who's behind this?"

Merced lay sullen.

Tap kept the rope pulled tight and began to tug Merced into more cactus.

"It's DelGatto!" Merced screamed in pain. "He's the one that got wind of this deal. He's been settin' it up for months. Now get me out of here!"

"Who shot Baltimore?"

"Hager."

"No. Who shot him with a .45?"

Again Tap tugged the rope tight.

"Wait! It was DelGatto. I told him not to do it!"

Tap climbed down off Brownie and hiked with gun in hand toward Merced.

"What are you goin' to do?"

"I'm thinkin' about shootin' ya."

"You cain't do that!"

"You know, Simp, I'm not really as nice a guy as you think."

Andrews yanked Merced up to his feet and shoved him off to the side. "If you run, I think you'll stay on your feet."

"What? Get these thorns out of my hands! I can't—"

"Sure you can!" Tap kicked Brownie, and they started at a gentle lope.

"Where we going? I cain't run all the way to Cheyenne!" he screamed.

"No, I reckon you can't. But maybe you can make it to the Denver Pacific tracks. They're only a couple miles away."

"What if I cain't make it?" Merced panted.

"Then I'll just have to drag you the whole way."

10

Simp Merced, bound hand and foot, lay across the tracks of the Denver Pacific Railroad, south of Cheyenne near the Colorado line. A distant column of smoke rose from the westbound train.

"Get me off here, Andrews! That train cain't stop in time!"

"Sure it can, Merced. He can see us for two miles."

"Us? You ain't laying out like a pig for the slaughter with your head on the tracks!"

Tap knew when he heard the train whistle that the engineer had spotted them. The roar of the oncoming train began to drown out Merced's screaming and yelling. When he saw the steam brakes kick in and the drive wheels freeze, Tap figured the train was going to stop.

But he had no idea if it could stop in time.

Whistles blew.

Brakes squealed.

Brownie shied away.

Merced fainted.

But the train slid to a stop twenty feet short of the bound man. The engineer and fireman met Tap with a string of shouts and curses. Tap had removed the marshal's badge from Simp Merced and now had it pinned to his own vest.

"Is he dead?" the fireman asked as he pointed to Merced.

"Nope. But he probably wishes he were."

"What do you think you're doin'?" the engineer screamed. "You can't stop a train!"

"I just did. Look, there's a gang that plans to hijack what you're carrying in that last car the minute you pull into Cheyenne."

"That's preposterous!" the engineer huffed. "We ain't got nothin' but mining equipment back there."

A man carrying a shotgun ran along the railroad cars toward them.

"You need an armed guard for mining equipment?"

The passengers strained to gawk out the windows.

"I want you to unhitch the engine, leave the cars here, and make a fast trip to town. I think we can stop this thing."

"I'm not about to do any such thing. Move that man off the tracks immediately!"

Tap's rifle was cocked and aimed at the engineer's head before the man could turn to run.

"What's goin' on up there?" the heavy man with the shotgun shouted as he puffed his way closer.

"Aren't you supposed to be back there guardin' that $500,000 worth of gold?" Tap challenged him.

The man looked startled as he stopped to catch his breath.

"What? I'm certainly not . . . You can't possibly think . . . How did you . . ." The man kept glancing back at the end car.

"Look, I need you to stay back there with the goods. I know you're takin' it into Cheyenne to trade for some Mexican silver. There's a gang in the depot waitin' for you."

The train's conductor huffed up to the group of men standing in the engine steam. "Abandon the train out here on the prairie? Absolutely not! We've a schedule to keep. Take that man off the tracks!" he ordered the engineer and fireman.

"I don't reckon I'll move much as long as that .44-40 is aimed at my head," the engineer replied.

"You don't have any idea who you're dealin' with! The Denver Pacific stops for no man!" the conductor insisted.

"Let me tell you what you're dealin' with. The westbound U. P. is supposed to hit Cheyenne in about thirty minutes. The plan was to rob both trains while they're in the station at the same time. A dozen well-armed men are there waiting for you."

"That's ludicrous. No one would dare such a stunt in a crowded city like Cheyenne."

Tap turned to the big man with the shotgun. "Have you got $500,000 worth of refined gold bars in that back car or not?"

"Actually . . . well, I assure you it is all a legal purchase and—"

"Look, mister, I don't give a hang what's goin' on here. All I know is that innocent people have been gettin' killed over this. I've got loved ones sitting in that terminal right now, and I'm goin' to do all I can to stop them from being injured. Now you stay here and guard your treasure, and I want to make a run for Cheyenne."

Tap noticed other passengers begin to cautiously debark the train.

"Don't listen to him!" Merced shouted. "I'm the acting marshal, not him!"

"What's going on?" the engineer demanded, his hands still raised.

"The engine's goin' on, that's what . . . Now get back there and unhook those cars."

"Who's the marshal anyway?"

"There's no law in Cheyenne," Tap admitted.

"I demand to know the meaning of all this!" the conductor fumed as the big man with the shotgun scurried back to his position in the last car.

"Mister, did you know Pappy Divide?" Tap asked.

"Yes. As a matter of fact, we were good friends, rest his soul." The conductor nodded.

"Good. You can tell him hello for me, because if you don't get this rig rollin', you'll be visitin' with Pappy a lot sooner than you thought."

"But you can't—"

"I'll send an engine back here to pick you up as soon as it's safe."

"What are you goin' to do with him?" The fireman pointed to Merced.

"Would it ruin your engine to run right over the top of him?"

"What?"

To a chorus of threats and curses from Simp Merced, Tap loaded him into the engine compartment. Within minutes the Denver Pacific engine, minus the cars, steamed north. Brownie loped riderless along the tracks. He dropped farther and farther behind the roaring 4-4-0 engine.

Pepper sat nervously in the baggage room of the Union Pacific terminal. Carbine Williams stared out a small crack in the door at the lobby.

"Tap will be along any minute now," he tried to reassure her.

"He was goin' to meet us here at three!"

"Well, he's still got five minutes."

"But if he needs me someplace in town, I should be there instead of waiting around here doing nothing."

"I figure he'll be here any minute. . . . Look out there!" Carbine nodded toward the waiting room.

Pepper peeked out the barely open door. "What is it? What do you see?"

"The one with the old black wool coat? That's one of the DelGatto bummers, and he's cradlin' a new lever-action repeater."

"Here? Are there others?"

"No . . . wait, there's one. One just walked in the door!"

"Why here? There's nothing to steal in a railroad waiting room."

"Unless they know somethin' we don't . . ." Carbine slipped the door closed and slid the heavy iron bar across the locking brackets. "I'm goin' through the back door and check out what's happening. You and Angelita look after Baltimore. You've got those guns that Tap left ya, ain't ya?"

"I'm going with you," Pepper announced.

"You can't. Someone needs to stay and look after Angelita and Baltimore."

Pepper started to protest and glanced over at Baltimore Gomez. "All right, but please hurry back and tell us what's going on."

Pepper fought the temptation to open the baggage room door

and peer into the lobby. She carried the shotgun in her hands as she paced the floor. Angelita stayed by Baltimore's side, a revolver in her lap.

A loud explosion some distance away rattled the windows that faced the tracks. Pepper could hear people in the lobby shout and run into the street. There was a second blast, then a light knock on the back door of the baggage room. Instantly the shotgun flew up to Pepper's shoulder.

"It's me . . . Carbine. . . . Open up," came a whisper.

She cracked the door and let the deputy in. "What happened?" she asked in a low voice.

"Another explosion and fire."

"Where?"

"The first one looked like it was down toward the Amsterdam Hotel. The second one could have been over by the Cheyenne Club."

"What's going on in this town? It's falling apart."

"I figure it means this gang is goin' to rob a bank or something, and the explosions are a diversion."

"Which bank? I thought some of the gang is out here in the lobby."

"The whole gang is here, and they're the only ones that didn't run."

Angelita came over to the back door where they were standing. "Maybe they're goin' to rob the train. The Denver Pacific will be here in a few minutes, and the Union Pacific rolls in at ten after. It's pretty hectic with both of them arriving at the same time. I ought to know—I'm down here every day."

"With the whole town putting out fires, there's no tellin' what they're goin' to do."

"Where's Tap? Tap ought to be here. . . . It's three o'clock!" Pepper fumed.

"The D. P. ought to be here!" Angelita added. "It's never late except for snow." She walked over to the one window in the room and peered down the tracks. "Here it comes!"

"Get away from that window. Come over here," Carbine called. "Wait until the train pulls up. Then we'll load up out the back door," Carbine instructed. "Maybe you two ladies should travel to Denver just to get out of town."

"We'll meet Tap on the east side of town, just like we promised," Pepper insisted. "But I sure wish he was here."

Carbine kept back in the shadows of the darkened baggage room and glanced out toward the Denver Pacific tracks.

"What in the world? There's only an engine! Tap's on that train!"

"He's what?" Pepper gasped.

"I'm goin' back out there. Lock the door behind me," Carbine ordered. "This is getting crazier by the minute!"

"I'm coming out too," she insisted.

"Mrs. Andrews," Angelita cried, "I don't think my father's breathing. Daddy!"

"But . . . I have to . . . Tap's . . ."

Carbine slipped out the back door with his pistol in his hand, and Pepper spun around to face Angelita . . . then back at the door.

"Please!" the girl cried.

Lord, I can't do it. . . . I can't do two things at once. I just don't know what . . .

She felt a gentle breeze and glanced about to see if Carbine had shut the door. The room was closed up, but Pepper hurried to Angelita's side. A quietness of spirit swept through Pepper, in such sharp contrast to her previous feeling that she was afraid she was about to faint. Tenderly she held the girl and kissed her forehead, at the same time gripping Baltimore's wrist.

"Honey, it must have just been the medicine. They said it would put him to sleep."

Several shots were fired outside the station, and Angelita jumped.

Pepper didn't.

"Put your hand right here," she instructed the young girl.

"What's happening out there?" Angelita asked.

"Mr. Andrews can take care of that. Can you feel that pulse?"

"Yes!" Angelita whimpered.

"Now you sit right here, and I'll be back. Is it all right if I leave you now?"

Angelita nodded her head. She had her left hand on her father's wrist and her right hand on the pistol in her lap.

Pepper slipped out the back door. Two more shots were fired. There was plenty of yelling from the front of the depot. A rough wooden ladder nailed to the outside of the depot baggage room seemed to lead to a small balcony in front of a false dormer window facing the tracks. With the shotgun in one hand, she began cautiously to climb the ladder.

"'O God, our help in ages past, our hope for years to come, our shelter from the stormy blast, and our eternal home.'"

The melody of the old Isaac Watts hymn trickled through her mind even as she pulled herself up into the little balcony and surveyed the scene below.

Spotting at least two fires burning in Cheyenne as they approached, Tap ordered the engineer and fireman to enter the train yard at the highest speed they could and still slow down at the depot. With wheels churning and whistle blaring, they roared into town.

As they approached the depot, he spotted several armed men on the loading dock. The engineer locked his brakes, and the train slid on the rails.

"Just as you get to the depot," Tap yelled to the engineer, "throw it back in gear, and don't stop until you get to the roundhouse. Once you get down there, throw it in reverse, and drive back out on the prairie to your train!"

"Are you kidding?" the engineer hollered.

"Do it!"

"What about the robbery?"

"That's my problem!"

Tap yanked Merced to his feet just as they pulled even with the baggage dock, about seventy feet short of the main terminal. Then suddenly he leaped from the moving train, dragging Merced with him.

With his hands still bound behind him, Merced bounced and flopped like a mail sack as he hit the rough wooden loading dock.

Tap rolled over once and came up on his haunches with his revolver in his hand.

His dramatic entrance went almost unnoticed as several bummers tried to run down the train engine that now chugged off toward the roundhouse. The only one who spotted his daring arrival was Carbine Williams.

"Tap . . . what in the world's goin' on?"

"They're tryin' to rob two trains at once! Can you get around to the east side? Where's Pepper and the others?"

"Safe in the baggage room."

"When's the U. P. due?"

"Any minute now."

"If you get a chance, stop her short of the station."

Carbine Williams sprinted east across the tracks, giving a wide berth to the depot.

Tap jerked Simp Merced to his feet.

"I'll kill you, Andrews!"

Tap shoved him on down the loading dock toward the main terminal.

"Let's go visit DelGatto!" he growled.

"You're tough, Andrews . . . but you're also stupid. Alex DelGatto's got a dozen armed men in that depot. They'll shoot you on sight!"

"There aren't two in the bunch that ever shot a gun when they were being shot at. I'll take my chances."

He held Merced by the collar of his coat and kept the Colt .44 pointed at the shorter man's head. Several of the gang abandoned their effort to chase the Denver Pacific engine. Most now ran back to the depot.

"DelGatto!" Andrews yelled. Several of the bummers backed away from their position as Andrews marched to the loading dock in front of the main terminal, using Merced as a shield. "Where's DelGatto?" he hollered at one of the men hiding behind a stack of baggage, with a new '73 Winchester carbine pointed at Tap and Merced.

"Mister, you're in the wrong place at the wrong time! You ain't got a prayer of gettin' out of here alive."

Tap's bullet blasted the wooden nail barrel next to the man's head. The bummer dropped his gun and bolted toward the depot.

Meanwhile Carbine Williams inched his way forward on the east. In the distance, the westbound U. P. train's whistle blew.

"DelGatto . . . I've got your boy Merced out here!"

Tap made sure Simp Merced was standing between his location and the depot.

"It's all over, DelGatto. I know about the $500,000 in gold. And Merced told me all about La Plata del Palicio Aztec. You don't get anything! You wasted your time. Ain't that a kick? You boys don't get a dime!"

"What's he talkin' about?" one of the bummers shouted. "Even if the gold don't come in, we still get that Mexican silver, don't we?"

"All you boys will get is about six months in jail. Unless you start shootin'. Then I'd say those who live through it will spend the rest of their lives in the Territorial Prison."

"I ain't doin' this if I don't get paid," one of them shouted.

"Wait!" DelGatto's high-pitched voice shrieked from inside the terminal. "He's just tryin' to scare you! Listen . . . that's the U. P. It's comin' in, and those riches will be ours. Finish him off, boys!"

"He's got Merced!"

Alex DelGatto peeked out from behind a beam at the entry to the waiting room.

Come on . . . just a little more . . . another step.

"Give up, DelGatto. I know that you're the one who shot Baltimore with a .45!"

"Shoot him!" Merced screamed. "He's ruined our plans! Shoot Andrews!"

"It's ruined, all right!" DelGatto yelled. "Two years of planning is ruined by a two-bit deputy."

"Shoot him!" Merced kept screaming.

DelGatto's voice began to taper. "Yeah . . . I'll shoot him."

The trail of smoke from Alex DelGatto's long-barreled .45 exploded into the air as Simp Merced slumped to the ground. Andrews fired one shot toward DelGatto's position and dove for cover behind a huge packing crate.

"You killed Merced!" one of the bummers shouted. "You killed your own man!"

"I've got no room for those who fail! Now kill Andrews!"

"I ain't goin' to wait and git shot by my own boss!" one bummer shouted. He threw down his gun and sprinted east, soon colliding with the barrel of Carbine Williams's revolver.

"That's right, boys," Andrews yelled, "if you don't aim to die right here, then throw those guns down and hightail it out of here!"

A couple more ran east and were laid down by a two-by-four-wielding Carbine Williams. Tap knew several were running out the front door of the terminal. He could hear gunfire, shouts, and curses.

They've taken to shootin' each other, I suppose. I know where DelGatto is, but I haven't seen Strappler anywhere.

Tap signaled for Williams to circle back around to the street side of the depot. He drew a bead on the open door, trying to stay protected by the shipping crates.

With Carbine around at the front, there was no signal for the incoming train to stop short, and the Union Pacific from Omaha slid, rolled, steamed, and whistled its way right up to the station.

Suddenly Alex DelGatto burst through the doorway. His left hand gripped Angelita's shoulder, and his right held a gun to her head.

Oh, Lord, no! This is insane. It's beyond money. Beyond revenge!

It's got to stop.

Right here.

Right now.

Oh, Lamb of God, who taketh away the sins of the world, have mercy on us!

"Throw it down, Andrews," DelGatto ordered. "I'll kill her. You know I will. Throw that gun down!"

Angelita grimaced from DelGatto's grip. She held her right hand in front of her stomach with all five fingers extended. Slowly, she hid the thumb, then the forefinger . . .

She's giving me a countdown!

"I said, drop it, Andrews!" DelGatto screamed above the roar of the train.

I surely hope we're communicatin', darlin'. 3—2—1!

When Angelita's last finger disappeared into her fist, she dropped straight to the floor, the weight of her body breaking her free from the gunman's grip. Startled, DelGatto fired wildly. The bullet flew over a pullman carload of passengers. Tap fired his .44 hitting DelGatto under the left eye. He cocked the pistol and raised it for another shot when a shotgun blast from the roof behind him caused him to turn and dive for cover.

Strappler, no more than twenty feet behind him, lay writhing in pain. A shotgun blast had ripped into him between the belt and the boots.

"Pepper!" Tap stared up at the tiny balcony in front of the dormer window.

"He was going to shoot you in the back!" she yelled out.

Suddenly she dropped the shotgun and slumped over the balcony rail.

"Pepper!" Tap screamed. "Pepper!"

No, Lord . . . no, no, no. You can't do this to me! No!

Tap ran to the ladder at the west end of the depot and climbed the steps two at a time. Swinging himself into the balcony, he lifted her off the decorative railing.

"Pepper, darlin' . . . honey?"

Her eyes blinked open. "I, eh, I got dizzy. I guess I fainted."

"Thank You, Lord!" Tap sighed. "It's all right. You can faint any old time you want—only next time don't do it from a balcony."

Her arms around his neck, his left hand around her waist, Andrews inched his way down the ladder. Once they reached the ground level, he carried her around to the main platform where Angelita stood next to Carbine Williams. The ten-year-old ran and threw her arms around both of them. Cheers and applause roared from the train as people began to debark.

"What's all this?" Tap mumbled.

"I guess they saw the whole thing," Carbine replied as he limped up to them.

A round-faced, thin-mustached conductor swung out of the railroad car clapping his hands.

"Marvelous! Marvelous! My, that was realistic! Splendid. The passengers enjoyed it immensely. What a dynamic concept. A street Mel-O-Drama to welcome folks to the West. Yes, yes . . . I must tell my superiors."

"A what?"

"Really, you must introduce the cast!" The conductor stepped back to the door and motioned for the passengers to continue to exit. Several ran over to shake Tap's hand.

"No, no," the conductor scooted them back. "First, ladies and gentlemen, we want to have an introduction of the cast."

"Cast?" Pepper swallowed hard.

Tap waved the crowd quiet.

"Folks, this is the West. It's not a game out here. Now if any of you are doctors, there's a couple of wounded men inside the waiting room. Strappler's got buckshot in his legs, and DelGatto is dead. We'll need a couple ambulances and an undertaker. It might be best if you hiked down there around the station to the east. We'll try to get the bodies gathered up as soon as we can. This isn't playacting. It's the real thing. Now, eh, welcome to Cheyenne, the Magic City of the Plains."

Men gasped.

Children cried.

Women fainted.

It took two hours for troops from Ft. Russell to restore any sort of order to the city. Six gang members were in jail. DelGatto and Merced were in coffins. Strappler and three others were in the hospital. The Denver Pacific had brought in its cars and was about ready to depart. The mayor and several city councilmen sat in the terminal along with Andrews and Carbine Williams.

Angelita and Pepper were inside the baggage room as Dr. Herbert Smythe, recently of Boston, examined Baltimore Gomez.

The door swung open, and Angelita skipped out with a smile

that revealed her beautiful white teeth and a dirt-smudged tear streak that ran from her cheek to her chin.

"Daddy's doing superior! Dr. Smythe said the medicine they gave him at the hospital helped him sleep through everything! Guess what else? Dr. Smythe is on his way to Denver too! He said he'd ride with Mr. Williams and Daddy just in case he could be of help!"

"That's the best news I've heard all day!" Tap smiled. "Carbine, go help the doc get Baltimore loaded up. That Denver train has got to pull out in a hurry if it wants to be close to keepin' its schedule."

"Oh, he can't go in there yet!" Angelita shouted.

"Why not?"

"Mrs. Andrews is gettin' an exam."

"She's . . . wh-what?" Tap stuttered.

"She told the doctor about being dizzy and stomach-sick lately, and he offered to give her an exam."

"Look, Andrews," Mayor Breshnan interrupted, "the council is quite serious about that offer. We'll provide you and Mrs. Andrews with lodging at a hotel "

"What about me?" Angelita interjected. "I'm with them."

"Yes . . . yes, the little girl also. And all your meals plus—"

"I'm not a little girl," Angelita insisted.

The mayor flashed an annoyed look at her. "Plus we will pay you one hundred dollars just to stay until June first."

"I'm not interested."

"Two hundred dollars?"

"Nope."

"This is highway robbery. You don't . . ."

One of the councilmen nodded his head and cleared his throat.

"All right," the mayor continued, "three hundred dollars. But that's our last offer."

Pepper was still buttoning the sleeves of her dress as she strolled out of the waiting room. The sparkle in her eyes, the sheen of her blonde hair, the glow of her cheeks contrasted with the worry and anxiety of the past several days.

She slipped her hand into Tap's.

"You ready to go, darlin'?" he asked.

"Yes. I believe everything's still loaded in the wagon. Angelita, you'd better go kiss your daddy goodbye."

"What about that marshal position, Andrews? What's your answer?"

"Mayor . . . it really isn't personal. I'm just not the right one. You keep Cheyenne, and we'll find a little more breathin' room out on the prairie. It just might be that the best thing you ever did was fire me. Come on, darlin', let's get loaded up."

"Tap, I need to talk about—"

"On the trail, Pepper honey. We've got the rest of the afternoon to visit." He ushered her out the front door of the building just as a flood of passengers swarmed the depot.

It took another half hour for all the goodbyes to be said and the Denver train to pull out. Finally Tap, Pepper, and Angelita drove east out of Cheyenne. Onespot and a tired Brownie were tethered to the back of the buggy.

The sun dropped far behind their shoulders, and a springlike breeze blew up from the south.

"It's like a horrible, heavy load bein' lifted off my shoulders." Tap sighed.

"You mean, leaving Cheyenne?"

"No, that whole Hager-Merced-DelGatto confrontation. For the past week it's been like a boot heel crushing me down. Did you know there wasn't even any Mexican silver on that train?"

"Really?" Pepper held onto his arm and laid her head on his shoulder. Angelita sprawled across them both with her head mainly in Pepper's lap.

"The railroad agent said they must have confiscated the goods at the border."

"So there was nothing to rob on the train?"

"Not on the U. P., but the Denver train did have $500,000 dollars' worth of gold."

"Will there be a reward for saving that gold?" Angelita piped up.

"No. No one will want anyone to know what kind of a scheme he was involved in."

"Well, I, for one, will miss that big U. P. Station," Angelita interjected. "It was a nice place to work. Did I show you this?" She held up a twenty-dollar gold piece.

"Where did you get that?" Tap asked.

"I sold the doctor the authentic pistol that fired the bullet that killed Mr. Merced."

"You sold the doctor DelGatto's .45?"

"Yes. He certainly didn't need it anymore. And this time I didn't lie!"

"Oh . . . the doctor! Listen, darlin', did he give you anything to help you feel better?"

Pepper continued to lean on Tap's arm and stared out ahead of the wagon. "No. He said there was nothing he could do."

"It's kind of what we figured then?" Tap nodded. "Just one of those things you got to live through, right?"

"Yes, I suppose that's one way to look at it."

"What'd he figure? A couple weeks of feelin' poorly? That cold last winter surely lingered in my chest for weeks."

"I'm afraid it will last more like nine months," she said softly, but she could feel each word butterfly in her stomach.

"Are you kidding? What kind of cold is that? Didn't he have any medicine you could—"

Angelita sat straight up. "I don't believe this! Mrs. Andrews, you married the world's dumbest man!"

"He is a little dense about some things," Pepper teased.

"Dense? What are you two—"

"Your wife is with child, you dolt!" Angelita hollered.

Tap yanked the reins back and stopped the wagon in the middle of the Pine Bluffs road.

"I'm going to have a baby?" he shouted.

"Well, I believe I'll be doing most of the work." Pepper grinned.

"A baby! I told you . . . I told you you could still have a baby! Didn't I tell you?"

"Yes, well, it isn't here yet. And I warned you, I might not be able to carry it the full term."

Tap slapped the reins, and the wagon lurched eastward. "I can't believe I'm going to be a father!"

"Well, I certainly hope it's not a girl!" Angelita piped up.

"Why?" Pepper laughed.

"Let's face it, Mrs. Andrews, he really doesn't understand women, now does he?"

"Maybe he'll learn," Pepper commented.

He held the reins with one hand and squeezed Pepper with the other.

"Mrs. Andrews, did I ever tell you you're the most beautiful woman in the world?" Tap beamed.

"Why, yes, Mr. Andrews, I believe you did mention it once or twice."

"Oh, brother! Are you two going to kiss?"

"There's a real good chance of it." Pepper laughed.

"On the lips?"

Tap ruffled Angelita's hair. "Yes, but you can hide your eyes if you want to."

"Are you kidding? Now we're finally getting to the good part."

For a list of other books by
Stephen Bly
or information regarding speaking
engagements write:

Stephen Bly
Winchester, Idaho 83555